THE LAST "LOCK THE DOOR" DREAM

D. R. SCRIBNER

CHAPTER 1

*H*er words struck me like a bolt of lightning. My core was shaken when the truth at last came out.

It was Sunday and I was feeling tense after hearing my mother and father having a loud argument. I locked the door to the bathroom and turned on the bath water. As I settled into the warm water, I relaxed. I thought about leaving Dent and moving to San Francisco. I had just received word a few days before that I had been accepted into San Francisco College. My graduation date from high school was only days away.

There had been a drought in the Dakotas for the last two years and my parents were having a hard time meeting family expenses. The stress of the drought caused my father to direct even more abuse towards me. There were also more arguments between my mother and Jeff, my father. It was during this time, while soaking in the water, I became uneasy. This uneasiness morphed into a feeling I'd had before some years ago. We were having dinner when I looked at my father from across the dining table and I wondered if Jeff Reed was really my father. I didn't think much about it at the time. This notion again popped into my head as I was soaking in the bath. I had no physical characteristics similar to his. Perhaps now, I thought, was the time. I should broach this idea with my mother. I would wait for the right time to confront her about this.

"Charles, your breakfast is ready," my mother yelled up to me.

"OK, I will be right down," I said.

It was Saturday and my father had gone into Dent for supplies. This was a good time to finally talk about Jeff, I thought.

"Mother, I have a question and I would like for you to give me an honest answer," I said.

"What is the question?" she replied.

"Is Jeff Reed my real father?" I asked.

At that moment, my mother's face went ashen. She started to tremble.

"Why would you ask such a question?"

"I don't look like him," I said. "He doesn't seem to have any love for me."

She sat there staring at me for quite some time. I had never seen her in the state that she was in now. Her ashen face and trembling body gave me a sense of foreboding. At last, her words came and the revelation of what she said would alter my life going forward. It would also cast a cloud over the way I felt about my mother.

"No, Charles, Jeff is not your biological father."

I sat there wondering what I should say and do after this revelation. Her words came crashing down on me. The world I knew had been transformed into a different place and time. The psychological problems I sensed I had were now multiplied by this new realization.

"Why didn't you tell me sooner?"

"I know I should have," she said.

All the abuse I had suffered over these years by Jeff cascaded upon me like a waterfall rushing to nowhere. The name-calling and cursing at me now made sense. My shaking body turned to anger towards my mother for holding this secret from me for such a long time. My mind exploded with questions about my biological father.

"What is his name?"

"John Alexander. We met in college and were together for only a few months."

"So, you were pregnant when you married Jeff?"

"Yes."

"Does Jeff know?"

"Yes."

"Did John know that you were pregnant with his child?"

"No," she replied.

All of a sudden, she rose from her chair and went into her bedroom. After a few minutes, she returned with a picture. It was a picture of her with John. I could tell from the picture that I did have similarities to him, especially our eyes.

"What did he major in while he was in college?"

"Engineering," she said.

"Do you know where he went when he left college?" I asked.

"I believe he went to Los Angeles."

At this time, I heard Jeff's truck pull into the driveway. I rose from my chair and went to my room. My feeling at this time was that I didn't want to see Jeff again. At the same time, I knew now what I had to do. *I had to try and find my biological father.* I also knew it would not be easy after all these years, but I had to try. Getting my education and finding my real father would be the main goals for me in the coming years. *In due course, these two things must be resolved.*

My departure from Dent was emotional for me. Jeff and my mother drove me to the bus depot in Dent. I sat on the far side of the seat in his pickup truck. I was wondering how or if I should say goodbye to him. I opened the door of the truck and retrieved my luggage. The door was still open. I looked in and gave my mother a kiss, I looked at Jeff and he looked away. I shut the door and made my way inside the depot.

The more than two day trip from Dent to San Francisco gave me time to reflect on the knowledge about John Alexander. It was also a time to think about Jeff Reed and what I would need to do to somehow reach an accord in my mind with the fact he was not my father. I began to wonder if my mother told him that I knew he was not my father. The fact he looked away without saying goodbye was an indication that my mother had told him.

My seat on the bus was toward the back and I had the seat all to myself. The weather was starting to turn cold and there was supposed to be a snow storm coming in from Canada. I was glad I would not have to face these snow storms again. After a few hours of riding, it became dark. I put my head back on the seat and went to sleep.

Before I left, my mother presented me with fifteen hundred dollars in cash. I was startled at this and was grateful to her. It did mitigate, to some extent, my feeling toward her in light of her not telling me about John Alexander. I knew it would not be easy for me to get my education while having to work, but I was going to try. Before I left Dent, I contacted the college about part-time employment and they said they had jobs available. This gave me hope.

I sent a note to my friend Lou Ames who was living in the Bay Area and told him I was coming to San Francisco. He sent a note back and said he was looking forward to seeing me. Lou was my best friend in Dent. He was a year ahead of me in high school.

After I got settled in San Francisco, I looked up my friend,

Lou. During one of our visits together, I opened up to him about how I was doing.

"I don't feel well," I said.

"What do you mean?"

"I don't know. I have these weird dreams. Like — I'm supposed to lock a door against an onslaught. But I *can't*. It devastates me instead. And then, once I wake up, I can't get out of bed for days! This week has been the worst."

"You ever think about talking with someone about this? You know this is not the first time this has come up. Remember when you yelled at me in high school that you were not crazy? I felt then you should be seeing someone," Lou said.

"I couldn't fully grasp the problem then, but I have since started thinking there is something really wrong."

I felt uncomfortable with the conversation. I blushed. I regretted bringing up my problems with him again.

"There is something else, Lou."

"What else?"

"I found out that Jeff Reed is not my real father."

"What?" Lou gasped.

"I have been meaning to tell you for a while now, but I just didn't know a good time," I said.

"Do you know who your real father is?"

"Yes."

"Who is it?"

"His name is John Alexander," I said.

"So have you tried to find him?"

"I have tried to find him but I couldn't."

"You really need to talk to someone about all this," Lou said. "Listen, I have been dating this person for about six months, and she has been seeing a psychologist for about a year, and she really likes her," he said.

"Really?" I said.

I wanted to drop the conversation. I sweated, thinking of the notion of talking to anyone about this. Or even of having a girlfriend.

"I can't imagine dating anyone, myself," I said. I was trying to distract him by veering the conversation in another direction. I then realized I wasn't veering at all, but rather I was beginning to see the heart of the matter. Unless I saw someone about what these crazy dreams were telling me, I couldn't see anyone romantically or succeed in any other area of my life. "OK. Do you know the name?"

Lou paused for a while and said he thought her name was Dr. Law.

"You should call her. I will get you the number."

"Maybe I will call her sometime. It appears you can't help me," I teased.

"I think you should," Lou said with a serious look on his face.

Lou was pretty perceptive, and I knew he remembered some of the things I told him when we lived in Dent, especially when I insisted I was not crazy. Now with the new realization about my father situation, Lou was especially concerned that I needed to talk to someone.

The idea of seeing a psychiatrist was foreign to me. Growing up in a small farm community, the notion of seeing a psychologist was not something I could imagine doing. This was not something people in Dent would do. If you had a problem, you just dealt with it, like Jeff Reed did.

All the signs of emotional upheaval from Jeff Reed were never treated. He took his rage and projected it onto my mother and me. He was closed to any kind of psychological help. His rage that he thrust on us was the main reason I felt the need to seek help. I needed someone who could understand my mood swings and the feelings of inferiority that I was experiencing. Perhaps I could find out about my bizarre dream patterns, as well. I often felt my life was at a standstill. Many times, my life became immobilized without a sense of direction.

As an example of my problems, on one occasion I got angry with Lou on the phone for no reason. I just blew up at him. I was sure this was the kind of behavior Lou was hinting at when he suggested I needed help.

After much soul-searching and wavering about seeking help, the need to explore the inner workings of my problems became a driving force for me. I knew with all the problems of my past, the discovery about John Alexander compounded the need to explore these other issues, which were literally blowing my mind apart. I would never be able to achieve my goals of being successful if I failed to solve these problems. It was because of these raging internal feelings that I decided I needed help.

After graduation from college, it further seemed like I had not resolved the issues confronting me. I did remember the name that Lou had given me some years ago. I began thinking about giving Dr. Law a call. Because I was busy trying to get established in a job, it took me more years to finally make the call. I was still having bizarre dreams and I was still having trouble feeling comfortable within myself.

After finding Dr. Law's phone number that Lou had given me a number of years ago, I did wonder if she was still in practice. I nervously picked up the phone and dialed.

"Dr. Law's office, may I help you?"

"Yes, I would like to make an appointment with Dr. Law."

"Can you hold for a minute?"

The person I was talking to sounded sexy. Sometimes, a voice can turn you on in an instant. It is like when you see someone for the first time and a spark happens. I was sensing this spark from hearing her voice. I wondered what this person would be like in person.

"May I have your name?" she asked when she came back on the phone.

"Charles Reed."

"Dr. Law can see you on Friday at 5 PM. Is that time okay with you, Charles?"

I began feeling anxious about this upcoming appointment as soon as I finished the call. I was unsure about the consequences of what I'd just done. *It is done now*, I thought. I took a deep breath and carried on the rest of the day.

It was becoming harder and harder for me to function on a daily basis. I would often be gripped with a complete sense of failure. I was completely immersed in myself and found it hard to relate to others. I was becoming more isolated and withdrawn. Sometimes, I would begin shaking uncontrollably.

On reflection, Lou was right all along about the notion of seeking help. He knew years ago that I had problems. Sometimes, it takes so much time to realize the need to seek help. The realization that you have a problem is a crucial first step to solving it. I recall reading something about that. It wasn't that I was unaware of the problems I had, it was just that the solutions were always put off for one reason or another. The call to Dr. Law was a call I should have made many years ago. I also began wondering why my mother did not recognize I had problems at the time. The fact she did not tell me about John Alexander until I was a teenager did not help. I began thinking whether she could have helped me unravel what was going on at the time, especially since she knew about John Alexander.

When Friday arrived, I was very anxious. I began wondering how the process would unfold. The question I kept asking myself was, would I ever find contentment within myself? Would the time ever come when I could be confident in my ability to relate to people?

CHAPTER 2

*D*r. Law's office was located in San Francisco. The building was a two-story brick building located on Fillmore Street. There was a person behind a glass encasement, and she smiled when I came in. After I told her my name, she told me to take a seat and that Dr. Law would see me momentarily.

While waiting to be called, I found myself trying to unscramble a picture on the wall. My mind became engrossed with the picture. The picture itself had varying colors going in every direction. I found myself reading all kinds of things into it. I tried to see if I could make something out of the wispy, flowing lines.

The more I studied the art, the more I began seeing faces. I could see different kinds of faces with large teeth and watery eyes. I saw a vortex which seemed to sink into oblivion. My body trembled at what I was seeing.

The memories of my childhood crashed down on me. The cold nights in North Dakota became vivid to my senses. I saw the Missouri River groping its way south. I heard the lovemaking in the next room by two people who fell out of love years ago. There was also the smell of alcohol permeating the house, along with the smell of bacon in the early morning hours when the chores were about to start. My aching body in the early morning was seeking a way to survive the eventual abuse that I knew was coming. My mind was imagining these things. I wondered about this kind of art. I wondered if the art was presented to invoke such an effect. The effect the art had on me was quite surprising. Why did the picture create such a response?

After studying the picture, I began thinking about this first visit. My foot twitched. Uneasy with myself, I was absorbed in the moment.

"Mr. Reed?"

I felt a little spooked by the interruption, as my mind snapped back to reality.

"Yes," I replied.

"Dr. Law will see you now."

God, I thought, *this is it.*

"Thank you," I replied.

I guessed this was Dr. Law's assistant.

"Were you the one I talked to on the phone?" I asked.

"Yes."

"You have a nice voice," I said.

"Thank you."

"I don't normally answer the phone but Joan, the receptionist, was out."

"What is your name?" I asked.

"Debbie."

Debbie was very attractive. She had long, dark hair and a shapely body with long legs and well-formed breasts. She did create an arousal in me. In my mind, I felt the whole process was getting off on the right foot.

"What kind of work do you do?" I asked.

I was just trying to make small talk until Dr. Law would see me.

"I am Dr. Law's associate," she replied.

I wonder what that means, I thought as we walked down to Dr. Law's office. I would find out eventually. Debbie knocked on Dr. Law's door.

"Come in," Dr. Law said.

I reached down and turned the door knob until the door was open and I was standing in the doorway.

"Yes, please come in," she said.

She rose from her seat and greeted me with a warm handshake. Her hand felt calm and reassuring against my moist and nervous grip. She gave me a slight smile and made me feel comfortable. I wondered how this would turn out. I suspected the voyage would be long and painful, but just maybe, she could help me. I felt relieved that I had taken this first step. As I have heard many times, it is the first step that is always the hardest. The first step is the realization that you have a problem and that you are taking measures to deal with it. I felt like I made the right decision. *Time will tell,* I thought.

Dr. Law's office was filled with diplomas and psychological pictures of the kind in the waiting area. One of the pictures was hung directly behind her and one was on the wall to my left. There was also one behind me. The pictures themselves were quite large but not out of proportion for the room. The pictures dominated the office decor. She did not have a desk. She had a small table with a phone on it. She sat in a simple couch chair. My seat was a little to one side of hers and was comfortable. It was a pillowed chair. The office itself was not large. It was about the size of a small den. It was not ostentatious but simple and to the point. Except for the pictures, the office was very white. I wondered why so much white. The cascading affect of the colors of red, green, blue and pink coming from the pictures gave the room a warm feeling.

"Mr. Reed," she said.

"Yes," I replied.

Dr. Law seemed to be a no-nonsense type of person. Very little emotion showed through. She was not a cold person, though. My guess was she was in her mid forties. Her hair was dark with a slight trace of gray. She wore her hair in a bun. She was wearing a blue and gray suit. She was of medium build and was well proportioned. She had brown piercing eyes. Her aura was one of sophistication and professionalism.

"Have you ever been in therapy before?" she asked.

"No."

"Well, our time together will be each Friday afternoon at this time. Is that okay with you?"

"Sure." *Hope this pays off,* I mused.

"Do you mind if I call you by your first name?" she asked.

"No."

Everything became silent. Five minutes went by.

"Should I say something?" I asked.

"What would you like to tell me?"

She was not taking notes.

"Are we being taped?" I asked.

"No. Why did you ask me that?"

"Just curious," I said.

I blushed.

Dr. Law watched me with a sense of objectivity. I was disoriented. I didn't know what I should say next. *Why am I here?*, I asked myself. "I am feeling uneasy right now."

"Why is that?"

"I don't know where to begin."

"Just begin."

"What do you mean?"

There was a period of more silence.

"I guess I am feeling frustrated with my life," I said.

More silence.

During this period, I became philosophical. I felt as though I could talk to Dr. Law. Perhaps this was the real first step. I began feeling empowered, even after this short time with her. Perhaps she was the one who could help me out of this quagmire I found myself in. The anxious moments that sometimes would subsume me might at last be solved. The journey might be long. The uncovering of emotions that were suffocating me may at last come to a resolution.

I was aware the therapeutic process was not for everyone. I knew it would require much soul-searching on my part. Inquiring into the mind can be bewildering and it requires discipline and a sense of wanting to get well. These were the kind of thoughts I was having about the process.

"Do you think you can help me?" I asked. Apprehensive, I had no idea why I asked her this at this time.

"I can try," she said.

With that, the process had begun.

I slowly recanted the story of my life. The abusive father and the times on the farm became the opening salvo for the process. She asked about my father and tried to explain that it was not my fault that he was like he was. It was then I told her that I found out that the father who raised me was not my real father.

"What do you mean?"

"My mother told me in my last year of high school that Jeff Reed was not my real father."

"What do you think about that?"

"I would like to find my real father."

"It has been quite a while since you found out. Have you tried to find him?"

"I have, but I have not had any luck."

"Did your mother tell you about him?"

"She only went with him for a few months."

"So, she really did not know him that well," she pointed out.

"Not that well."

Dr. Law also wanted to know more about my mother. She asked why I thought my mother put up with the abuse for such a long time. She asked me about my young years. "It seems like you have come a long way," she said.

I thought about that. I guess I had come a long way from Dent to San Francisco.

This first meeting was good. When I left, I was feeling much better. One of the main therapeutic notions from this first meeting was that I was taking the blame for my father. That, somehow, I felt it was my fault he was the way he was. It also became apparent that I also felt guilty that I could not protect my mother from his abuse. The discovery about Jeff Reed not being my biological father further exacerbated my problems.

The next Friday, she began to ask me more about my father and the trauma I felt about the discovery of John Alexander. I think she could tell I was getting nervous. I felt my hands getting sweaty. I was again blushing.

"How are you feeling?" she asked.

"A little nervous," I said.

There was more silence. She kept the same posture, never showing signs of what she was thinking. It was during this interlude that I thought about things outside of myself.

Some of the things I was interested in came rushing back to me since achieving some insight into the dynamics of my situation. Maybe this was because I began to realize that I was not responsible for my father. I was an innocent bystander in his abusive behavior.

"Thank you, Charles. The time is up for today. We will meet again next Friday, okay?"

"Yes, thank you."

The session had come to a close. I was feeling elated. I felt the guilt I had over these years was subsiding in the first few sessions.

Before I left, I said my goodbyes to Debbie. I was attracted to her.

"See you next time," I said.

"Thank you, Charles, see you next time," she replied.

The elective affinity on the phone now became a reality. I desperately wished I could see her more often, but I'd never date someone while I was in therapy — at least, not if that woman knew I was in therapy. How embarrassing would that be?

One of the questions Dr. Law asked me during one of my sessions interested me. The question caught me off guard. I reflected on the question. In my mind, it was important to really focus on what I wanted to do with my life. The crossroads of interest and ability had to be reconciled. *The exploration will now begin in earnest, as I grapple with the problems at hand. It will be a challenge.* I felt up to it. Just maybe, there was something in my dreams that held the clue going forward.

One of the dreams I had was as follows:

Debbie and I laughed and sang together. She wore a tight fitting red dress. It was sexy. I got aroused. I pulled her to me. I kissed and caressed her. I felt elated just to be with her. We explored each other. We were talking and dancing together. It was so delightful, the two of us as one. The lovemaking we shared was etched in my memory, even though it was just a dream.

The dream was filled with a true excitement and wonderment. It was my first love dream. The dream was not just about my love for Debbie, but also about the intellectual connection I had with her. I was captured by her piercing eyes. Her posture and the way she carried herself also evoked a deep arousal in me.

This feeling was solidified when I found out about her. She graduated first in her class at Stanford University, majoring in Psychology. These dual facets of intelligence and physical beauty became embedded in my mind.

The cure I was seeking was perhaps wrapped up with Debbie, rather than Dr. Law. It was hard for me to imagine this conclusion. I knew Debbie could not be my therapist, but I felt she could help me in areas that Dr. Law couldn't. I wanted Debbie to be my love. I needed someone to support me. Trusting another person, especially someone like Debbie, would be a dream come true. I felt so undeserving of her. This was the kind of problem I was hoping therapy would help resolve.

My confidence had been shattered years ago in Dent. I was determined I wanted to go further with my life. I wanted to achieve more.

"Charles?" called the receptionist.

"Yes," I replied.

"Dr. Law will see you now," Debbie said.

She looked fantastic. She was wearing a simple black dress which showed off her body completely. I was again struck by her poise and composure.

"Thank you," I replied.

"You know where the office is?" she asked.

"Yes."

Dr. Law was sitting in her chair waiting for our session to begin.

"How are you, Charles?" she asked.

"OK."

There was a brief silence. I was reflecting on what I was

going to discuss. I thought the first sessions went well. I felt relieved about the guilt that had been with me for my whole life. I was wondering if perhaps this could be the main reason I was shy and felt uncomfortable with others. I knew the therapeutic process was not easy.

After the first meeting, I thought about my past. I was trying to understand all the events which impacted my personality. The guilt I felt for all these years seemed on the way to resolution. Guilt is a strong emotion and can lead to suicidal thoughts. I learned about the guilt complex and what a powerful emotion it is when I read Freud.

She sat for a while and then she said the following: "Most sons want to be like their father." She went on to say that I could not be like my father. "You need to be your own person. The main goal we will be working on together is to make you a whole person. Right now you are dealing with different emotions, which need to be refocused and brought into a new reality. You must divorce yourself emotionally from him. You are already doing things differently. We will keep exploring this issue."

"You are talking about Jeff Reed, but how does John Alexander fit into the picture?" I asked.

"Yes, although John Alexander is your biological father, you were not raised by him. What I mean is, you must not be like Jeff Reed."

I sat there thinking about my situation and how to resolve the dilemma of emotional attachment. On the one hand, I knew she was right that I could not be like Jeff Reed, and on the other hand, I wondered if I were like John Alexander.

During this session I wondered if I should talk to her about my dream. I thought about it.

The dream unfolded as follows:

I stayed in a hotel in a large city, room 303, surrounded by skyscrapers. I went to the lobby and looked for a place to be seated but all the sofas were taken. I decided to go back to my room. I walked around the building trying to find my room, but I could not find it. I asked the person at the front desk where my room was. She said the room had been rented. I desperately shook. I had to get my things. My plane was leaving in an hour. It was night and very dark. I hailed a cab.

The drive was slow. Finally, we arrived at the airport. The plane was about to leave. I was in a state of panic. I frantically searched for my ticket before I finally found it. It had numbers all over it. There were complex numbers weaving in and out. I tried to figure them out. The plane was about to leave. I entered the cabin and took my window seat. The plane took off. It was flying very slowly four feet off the ground. We were soon flying over the ocean. We were still only four feet above the ocean. I could see the waves, even though it was dark. We flew to nowhere. I checked my ticket to see where I was going. The numbers were not decipherable. I again felt lost.

I woke up. The dream made me feel uneasy. Like some of the other dreams I had, I was sweating profusely when I awakened.

I wondered what the dream meant. I went over it with Dr. Law.

The following is how she interpreted it:

"Dreams can be difficult to interpret. The event about not finding a place to sit could be related to your shyness. You did not wait for a sofa seat. Not being able to find your room and your reaction to it, seems to strike at your insecurity. The airplane ride flying so close to the ground might be related to your need for more growth in your personality. More development and emotional progress is needed. The complex ticket information might mean you are trying to unscramble your emotional life."

I thought about what she said, and it seemed to make

sense. I would have to digest this analysis. I began to unwind the emotional baggage that had consumed my emotional self. Freeing the guilt component was a big discovery for me. I slowly started to feel better. I actually looked forward to the next session.

CHAPTER 3

Other than Lou and my sessions with Dr. Law, I found myself alone most of the time. Meeting Debbie gave a jolt to my life. Between getting the job at First Financial Group and meeting Debbie, life started to look up. I needed to make a date with her. I had to do it. *I must carry on.*

For some reason, Thursday was not a good day. I was feeling anxious and insecure. I felt my life was starting to change. Deep emotions were emerging. My unconscious self battled with my conscious self. Things I had repressed years ago tried to get out. *I must contain myself,* I thought. *I need to talk to Dr. Law. Let her help me.* I was drowsy.

It had been a long day. I took my clothes off and sat on the end of the bed. It was a queen size bed, which I purchased after I moved into the new apartment. It was comfortable, and the fluffy pillows I bought added to the overall comfort. I thought about Debbie. There were no blankets on the bed, just a white comforter and sheets on the bottom. It was very warm and cozy. Soon the process of winding down began. A never-ending cycle of dream patterns emerged.

Another dream unfolded as follows:

Thinking patterns started to get scrambled. Like the pictures in Dr. Law's office, colors became distorted. A dark abyss appeared, beckoning me to enter. I became confused. The kind face of my mother reassured me. *It's a black hole. I will never get out. I will be squeezed like a noodle. The event horizon is nearing. I don't see it, but I know it's there.* I felt the pull. *It's getting stronger.* People were flying by me. They were prodding me to enter. The dream continued. Debbie came into view. She was passing by me. She was nude. I grabbed her leg and held on. We were soaring together toward the black abyss. I was also nude. I started kissing her body. I was feeling gleeful and completely satisfied with her. I stroked her hair. Her flowing hair was soft to the touch. Her lips were full. Her lips were aflame with red lipstick. The interlude continued until we were making love. Together, as one, we continued soaring in the clouds. White fluffy clouds consumed us. The black abyss disappeared. I felt free.

Free from the torture of a lifetime, I did not want the dream to end. It was nice to have this dream about Debbie. *She will be my dream lover, someone I could cherish.* When I awoke, the bed was wet. I had been perspiring. It seemed to be a given that I would perspire while dreaming. I wondered if I would ever have her for real. This is what I wanted.

Friday had arrived and I found myself wondering what I should discuss in this session. Since a lot of the problems developed when I was young, I pondered what other elements of my personality needed analysis. *What further demons have to be revealed?* I asked myself. Was the abuse by my father the crux of the problem or were there other forces acting on me which were causing my unhappiness? Dr. Law said to me during one session that the time was all mine and I could talk about whatever I wanted.

I looked at the clock, and I knew my time was almost up.

"Is this bothering you?" she asked.

There was a period of silence.

"I think I am starting to forgive my father."

Dr. Law became much more attentive to me. She gave me a slight smile as the session was ending. It made me feel good.

"Our time is up. See you next time."

At this time, the thought of finding John Alexander was becoming a driving force for me, but I knew I had to carry on without him. *Someday, I might find him,* I thought.

When I was leaving the office, I noticed that Debbie was not there. Joan was there instead.

"Debbie's not here?" I asked.

"No, she left for another position."

Oh God, I will never see her again, I thought.

I didn't realize how upset I was, but it must have been noticeable to Dr. Law. It was during my next session that the topic of Debbie came up. I think when she saw me the last time she probably noticed how upset I was. It was as though she knew I liked Debbie. She must have been watching me when I left after my last session, or perhaps it was during the session that she noticed.

"You seem upset today. You seem a little flush. Is everything OK?"

"No, nothing is wrong."

I could not talk to her about my feelings for Debbie. All facets of the dream came to me. The facts of the dream came cascading into my conscious mind. The sexual overtones were evident. The event of making love to Debbie and the dark abyss, which accompanied the dream, came into focus. I needed to talk to Dr. Law about this; however I just did not feel right discussing Debbie at this time. *Perhaps another time I will deal with it,* I thought. But then, I had to find out where she was.

"I seem to have grown fond of Debbie," I said.

"I knew you liked her."

"Where is she now?"

"She took a position with the De Anza Hospital."

"Why did she leave?"

"She is doing her intern work to become a psychotherapist."

At this news, I became agitated. I was poised to ask her out, and now she was gone. I wasn't sure I even wanted to go to therapy again. I started to get a severe headache, and nausea swept over me. I had to be with her. She was becoming a part of my psyche, and the dreams I had of her indicated the deepening attachment to her that was emerging. Now she was gone.

The challenge now was to contact her at the hospital where she worked.

"How have you been, Charles?"

She was trying to get me back on point.

"Are you still embroiled with the poverty problem?" she asked, referencing my obsessive concern about the poverty problem that is gripping America.

"No," I replied.

"What do you think?"

For some reason, my mind swirled. "Life is funny," I said.

"What do you mean?"

"I just wonder what it is all about."

Time ticks by. Off to nowhere. Garbled thoughts permeate my words. How do I explain what's on my mind? Delving into neuron development with the genetic circuits and trying to understand the mapping of axons and dendrites which form the basic construct of the mental makeup of us all. These were the thoughts I had as I sat there. *Is the world predestined by the genetic information of our genome?* Passing along of information through the ages from beginning to end seemed so strange to me. The synapses of life sparked over billions and billions of times. The workings of life-form and the physics of the universe, from the beginning of time until the present, were thoughts that kept repeating in my mind. The billions and billions of stars and planets which make up our universe seemed so extraordinary to me. Thinking everything was going to be OK seems like a never-ending fantasy. I felt a sense a remorse for some reason. Was it possible that the unknowable could be known?

In the early morning hours, I became aware that time would never end. How is it possible that life could end but that time keeps moving into the unknown? Infinity is the doghouse of resolution, as it keeps the wonderment alive. The gods of the universe will not let us escape. We are trapped in a time warp moving forward. The field equations have been replaced by string theorists who think they have the answer to everything. We all want to know what the "it" is. It is elusive and not knowable. Material advances are but brief interludes to keep us happy for the moment. More on this later and we are guided by events which are yet to unfold. The asymptotic mapping always stretches to infinity. Points that don't touch seem significant. Let's talk later when the sun rises and we are confronted with more undiscovered problems. Lock the door, Charles, my mother would say. I looked at my watch, and there were only three minutes left of the session.

"Charles," said Dr. Law.

"Yes."

"Our time is up."

To get to the core of the problem becomes a new problem. WHEN WILL IT EVER END?

"See you next time," she said.

"OK."

I walked out of the office and gently closed the door. *At least I didn't ramble about mundane issues.*

CHAPTER 4

*I*t was Friday after another session with Dr. Law, when I decided to call Debbie. I knew it was a little late, but I felt I would take a chance and call. I nervously dialed her number at the hospital. I found myself shaking, wondering if she would even talk to me. It had been three months since I had spoken to Debbie in Dr. Law's office.

"De Anza Hospital," was the reply.

"May I speak to Debbie Winslow?"

"One moment, please."

There was silence for quite some time. I wondered if she would come to the phone. I was still nervous and anxious.

"Hello, this is Debbie Winslow."

"Debbie, this is Charles Reed. I am a patient of Dr. Law's. Do you remember me?" I asked.

I felt my voice sounded nervous and probably unsure. I was hoping she would understand my situation.

"How are you, Charles?" she asked.

"I am OK, How are you doing?" I asked.

"I am doing OK as well."

"Glad to hear everything is good with you," I replied.

There was again silence for a brief moment.

"What can I help you with?" she asked.

"I just thought I would call and see how you are doing," I said.

"That's nice of you, Charles," she replied.

"Debbie, I was wondering if we could get together some-time for coffee."

There was another brief silence before she answered.

"Let me think about it. I am really busy now, and I am not sure when I would be able to meet you. Perhaps you can call me sometime when I am not so busy. I must go now."

"OK, I understand."

As I hung up the phone, I felt like a complete failure. I just could not imagine that I would ever be with Debbie. I guessed I would have to give it more time. *Maybe someday*, I thought.

My mind raced. All the unknowns came crashing upon me, like waves in the oceans of a new day. I was interested in her professional career. How much longer did she have to go before she was a licensed professional, I wondered. It had been a month since I had last talked to her. I again was anxious about calling her. I didn't think I should feel so unsure of myself about Debbie. *Perhaps I need to get more understanding of what is happening about this.* I could not get her out of my mind.

The dream unfolded as such:

I walked down a long narrow road. It was late at night, and I could see lights coming from the distance. It appeared to be a large city, and the lights got brighter the closer I got. In front of the city was a large black door. It was ajar. I walked inside, and in front of me were stairs going upward. I started climbing the stairs. It seemed like I would never reach the top. After I finally reached the top of the stairs, I looked out and could see another lighted city. To my left and right were mansions of white marble. Farther down the road, there was a museum. There were large wooden doors which were closed. I had an urge to go in. I pulled on the metal handle, and the door opened. Inside the museum were pictures of various colored squiggly lines like the ones in Dr. Law's office. Toward the back of the museum, there was a large picture, and as I got closer to it, I could see it was a picture of Debbie.

I started shaking. I woke up. I tried to figure out what the dream meant. Museums were things of the past. I thought maybe Debbie should be in my past. Perhaps it was just an interlude in a young life going forward. On reflection, I just could not cope with this analysis. I was confronted with two things in my life that needed to be reconciled: The need for Debbie to be in my life and the other was to find John Alexander. Both were important to me.

"Hello, I would like to send a dozen roses to someone," I said to the florist.

"Yes, we can do that," was the reply.

"I would like to send a dozen roses to Debbie Winslow at the De Anza Hospital Psychology Department."

I felt relieved after placing the order of flowers. I could not give up on Debbie. I had to keep trying.

During my last conversation with Lou Ames, he suggested that perhaps I should hire a private investigator to try and find John Alexander. I had been thinking about this and maybe I should try this, I thought.

CHAPTER 5

$\mathcal{D}$eep in the woods, a shot rang out. The end had come. Few leaves fell at the sound of the blast. Serenity had soon settled into its rightful place. The spinning of the universe had no answer to what happened. The billions of stars in the solar systems made not a sound. The event was but a pebble in the ether. The solitude of that moment echoed loudly when it was over. The event was real, but few cared. The tragedy went unnoticed except for the occasional deer that would happen by. This will unfold in due course and you will see the answer.

"Hello," I answered when the phone rang.

"Charles?"

"Yes," I replied.

"This is Debbie."

"Hi Debbie, how are you," I asked.

"I want to thank you for the beautiful roses."

"Glad you like them," I replied.

"I wanted to tell you that I will be free this Friday, if you would like to get together."

I shuddered. My mind turned to jelly.

"Was there someplace you would like to meet?"

"There is a café near the hospital called Saul's," she said.

"Oh yes, I know where that is. What time can we meet?"

"How about 7:30 PM?" she said.

"Great, I will see you then."

Saul's was a place where many young people would go and talk and just hang out. It was rustic inside. There were several deco paintings on the walls. There was room for about twenty-five people or so, with wooden chairs and tables for two or four people and a long bench against the wall with padded seating. A candle on each of the tables created a nice glow and ambiance to the room. The menu was pretty all-encompassing, serving breakfast, lunch and dinner. Many people would stop in for coffee and bagels in the morning. Overall, it was a nice place to have a conversation. My guess was that Debbie went there after work sometimes.

I arrived at Saul's early. It was around 7:00 PM. I asked for a table near the end of the room. It was quiet and offered a good location to have a conversation. I sat on the side of the table so that I could see when Debbie arrived. Of course, I was again nervous about meeting Debbie. The anticipation of seeing her all week was almost more than I could bear. Now the time I had been hoping for was coming to fruition.

After about twenty minutes, Debbie came through the door. I rose from my seat and motioned to her. She started walking toward me. She was wearing a tight red dress, the same kind of dress she was wearing in some of my dreams of her. It definitely showed off her shapely body. She wore her hair down, and she looked wonderful. She was the most beautiful woman I had ever seen. It was hard for me to believe I would be seeing her. I wanted to take her in my arms and hold her and kiss her. Not only did I want to have her sexually, I also wanted her intellectually. It was a truly all-encompassing feeling. The kind of feeling one gets once in a lifetime. It was all before me now, as I watched her walk over to our table. At the same time, I wasn't sure what we should talk about this evening.

I needed to know more about her. In my mind, I needed to get past her beauty and explore her mind. All my emotions came upon me this night. The poor boy from Dent, North Dakota was about to fall in love. My lonely life could be changed forever. That was my hope, anyway.

"How long have you been here?" Debbie asked.

"Just a few minutes," I replied.

"It is nice seeing you again, Charles," she said.

"Nice seeing you again as well," I replied.

"How have you been?" she asked.

"Pretty well," I replied.

The conversation was light and airy. She talked about her new job. Her desire to get her PhD in psychology was upper-most in her mind. I let her talk.

She told me she was homeschooled by her mother until she went to college at Stanford. Her father was a medical doctor, and her mother was a librarian. She was an only child, like me. We had this in common, I thought.

Her foot rubbed against my leg under the table as she tried to get more comfortable. Occasionally, we would look fully at each other. After about an hour of trivial talk and background chatter, we finally started looking into each other's eyes. It seemed like a probing stare at first, but then it became more sensuous. *This could be the beginning of love,* I thought. I wasn't sure how she felt though.

She was a complex person. After an hour or so of talking, it seemed she was starting to feel more comfortable with me. She laughed more. Our eyes were becoming fixed with each other over a longer period of time.

With her background in psychology and my education in economics, maybe we could solve some of the world's problems. I wasn't expecting to solve any problems outright but maybe shed light on the periphery. I decided that this was not the time to bring this up. In fact, I thought she would probably find the whole area boring. I didn't know. *Another time*, I thought.

It became harder for me not to kiss her and hold her like in my dream. We had been at Saul's for over three hours. I didn't want the date to end. I kept trying to keep the conversation going. I began to talk to her about myself. The fact that I, too, was an only child was something I wanted her to know. She did have a way about drawing me out concerning my childhood and early life. I told her about the abuse at the hands of my father. I told Debbie that I often wondered if there was something I could have done to stop the abuse. I was reluctant talking to her about this. It was important for her to know about it, and it seemed that she would understand.

"Charles, there was nothing you could have done."

"I know, but I just feel so bad. This feeling of guilt just will not go away."

The evening went on like this. I wanted time to stand still. There was so much more I wanted to discuss with her.

She mentioned to me that she was having a little difficulty in trying to navigate her new position. She was reporting directly to a psychiatrist specializing in cognitive analysis. Her work toward her doctoral degree would probably take another year or so.

"Wow, I didn't know psychology was so involved," I said.

"Yes, it is quite involved."

I told her I was also interested in psychology.

"Maybe I will pursue a degree in psychology as well," I joked. She laughed.

"What do you do?" she asked.

I told her I worked for a financial company. "I put clients and investments together," I replied.

"Do you like doing that?" she asked.

"Well, I am having a good time so far."

We both looked around Saul's to see what was going on. There was a young black female playing the piano and singing this evening. *She is quite good*, I thought. The music she played was soft rock, and most of the songs were from the fifties and sixties. She played many Bob Dylan songs, which I liked. One of the songs she sang was "A Blossom Fell" by Nat King Cole. When she started singing, I reached over and took Debbie's hand. We stared at each other. We both experienced a moment of love for each other during the song. At least I thought that was the case.

"Beautiful song," she said.

"It is one of my favorites."

All in all, I thought the first meeting with Debbie went well. The elective affinity on the phone had now come full circle. For sure, I was falling in love. We continued talking for a while longer. Soon we encountered a quiet interlude. We both sat there with our thoughts. It was a reflective moment of our first time together. I was still unsure if I deserved her. I tried to make her comfortable. I let her talk. It was an equal give and take. We tried not to talk about the things that would divide us, like politics and religion. Both these areas would come at a different time. Finally, Debbie said she had to go.

"I so enjoyed our time together. Perhaps we can do this again," she said.

"I would love it."

"Call me next week."

"Will do, I enjoyed it," I said.

I remained seated as she got up from the table to leave. I walked around to where she was and hugged her.

"Can I walk you home?" I asked.

"Not tonight, I will just take a taxi this time."

"It was nice," I said.

"Lay, Lady Lay" by Bob Dylan was being sung. Beautiful, I thought. Debbie walked out the door into the night. Before she left, she looked back at me and gave me a short wave and smile. *THERE IS LIGHT AT THE END*, I thought. The unison of two people began to merge. *It will be easier to call her now.*

CHAPTER 6

The next week, I called Debbie.

"Hello," Debbie said.

"Hi, Debbie, this is Charles. How are you? I thought I would ask you for coffee or maybe get some dinner out."

"That is nice of you, Charles. I am afraid I won't be able to see you this week. I've had some issues at work which are taking more time than I would like."

"I'm sorry. Maybe I can call you next week, then. OK?" I asked.

"Yes, that would be fine."

After the call, I felt a little shaken. I hoped I didn't say something that upset her. I did think everything went well at Saul's.

The more I thought about things after I hung up the phone, I decided to go out on my own. I was a little upset about not seeing Debbie. I decided I would go to Jake's Bar and Grill on Union Street and have a glass of wine and do some thinking.

The walk home from Jake's to my apartment was about six blocks. The problem was, it was mostly uphill. At the last minute, I decided to hail a cab and go to the Marina. It was a warm night and the sun had not yet set, but it would not be long before its final phase would close another day.

I told the driver to drop me off by the grassy knoll. I walked across the knoll and sat on one of the benches which were located about five feet from the bay. The bay itself was glistening from the setting of the sun. Soon the glow of the moon came into view. The twin forces of nature were completing their nightly cycle. The eons of the now meshed into the oneness of the present. I was feeling the effects of its ending. The cycle of the present will be with us until the end of time. The expansion will continue.

I sat there contemplating my situation. I had not seen Debbie for a while. I wondered how she was doing. I determined, sitting there staring out at the bay, that I was not as happy as I wanted to be. I thought I needed to do some more thinking about this.

The sun was almost out of sight now and you could see its glow, bringing light to another part of the world. The moon was now at the forefront of light. It was beautiful now. Lights from the across the bay became the final glow, which were absorbed by the bay. The bay was now in its glory. The ebb and flow to eternity continues. The bay took center stage.

The effects of the wine had worn off, and I had to get back to reality. There were things brewing in my mind. Perhaps the therapy with Dr. Law was taking effect. *Maybe this unhappiness will pass*, I hoped.

The next meeting with Debbie was again at Saul's. We both seemed to like it there. Saul's was not as busy as the last time we met. Debbie was more talkative this time. She told me about an event that had an influence in her life.

While she was in high school, she had a boyfriend that she loved. His name was Todd and he was the "big man on campus." He was an athlete and all-round good student. They went together for almost two years until they both graduated high school. Debbie said Todd was in the army and was shipped off to Germany. They wrote each other every day for six months. They did plan to marry at some point. She told me Todd was killed in an accident. He was driving an army truck at a fairly high speed when he lost control and the truck careened down a steep embankment, killing him instantly. When he didn't answer her letters, she phoned his parents in their hometown, asking for any news they might have about him. They told her about the accident.

On hearing the news, she broke down in tears. She could not believe it. She mourned for months after getting the news of his death. Even now, she still cries from time to time. Even as we spoke, tears were falling down her face. The memories seemed vivid for her as she continued to tell me the story. "I don't want to bore you with my past," she said.

"That's OK, I understand," I said.

I could tell that Debbie was a loving person by the way she was talking about Todd. I felt sad about her experience. My heart ached for Debbie.

The conversation with Debbie stirred a feeling of remorse and other emotions about the end. The finality we all face. *What is the point of this life?* I wondered.

Debbie sat there looking so beautiful. She wore a blue dress, and it showed off her body completely. I told her again how sorry I was for the loss of Todd. I explained my feelings about life and death. "Life is so fragile," I said.

I began a soliloquy of the death scenario that I would often ponder. She seemed interested, so I continued. I didn't know if all this talk was appropriate. It was, it seemed to me, a little morose. After she told me about the loss of Todd, she seemed more settled. She started to relax. We both had some wine. The music again started up and was soft and had the effect of creating a nice environment for conversation.

"What are you thinking about, Charles?"

"It is a long story."

I became expansive in my conversation with Debbie. Maybe I had a little too much wine. I found myself talking about the dinosaurs and how they lived on the planet for over 175 million years. Why on earth I would talk about dinosaurs at this time was beyond me. I continued talking about them. "This is not the planet of man but the planet of dinosaurs," I opined.

I also became embroiled in this whole life and death thing. Most people think about life and death, I reasoned.

"I don't purport to know any of the answers. The whole notion of life and death has been a conundrum since the beginning of time. Philosophy has tried to answer many of the issues since man began to think. Religion also seeks to rectify the life and death notion," I said.

I further added that after finishing my studies and taking courses in Philosophy of Religion, I came to the conclusion that death was final and there was no afterlife. The creation of man, in my view, was an accident of nature. It was not something preordained. I could see though, because of the complexity of the human anatomy, why many people would look to these other sources for understanding and solace. The rationale for the beginning and end of life becomes an individual decision each of us makes. After much study and thought, I became aware that I was an agnostic. There was too much of the unknown that couldn't be explained.

I wondered if Debbie would think less of me for disclosing this fact. I felt she had to know sooner rather than later. Life is the essence of everything. Without life, there is a void. The imagination can run wild. We can form a model of what we think death is, but the uncertainty of it casts a shadow on the spirit. The afterlife becomes as one. Squiggly lines seem so pervasive in the scheme of things. The synapses have long vanished. The memories have long faded. We are now united as one. We are now a part of the ether. Peace has been granted.

"What are you thinking?" Debbie asked.

"Just what a nice time I am having," I lied.

There was a DJ at Saul's this evening. Usually they had live entertainment, but tonight they had a DJ. He was a young man in his twenties. He was of thin build and dark complexion and was wearing a white open shirt with black slacks. He had a winsome smile, and I could tell he was well-liked by the people.

A few of the couples started to dance to some of the slow music he was playing. I asked Debbie if she would like to dance. I put my arms around her waist and pulled her to me. I immediately became hard, which seemed to happen with Debbie. I was feeling embarrassed, but she didn't seem to mind. It was kind of difficult to control my emotions. I just so wanted to make love to her. I started to perspire, and I said we should sit down before the song ended.

"Is everything OK?" she asked.

"I am all right."

It seemed to me that I did most of the talking. I felt guilty about this. The night was getting late and I became tired and I was sure Debbie was ready to go as well.

"I think we should go now," Debbie said.

"Let's do it," I said.

When we got up to leave, the DJ started playing "Mona Lisa," by Nat King Cole. It was one of my favorite songs, a big hit in the early fifties. I opened the door for her, and we walked into the night. It was a warm night and the stars were out and the moon was full. We could hear the song for a while, and then it faded.

The walk to her flat was about eight blocks. On the way, we passed by Dr. Law's office. I questioned if I should talk to

Dr. Law about Debbie. There were other things I needed to discuss with her, like the death of my father and my unhappiness. *I have to figure this all out,* I thought. When we arrived at her flat, we both stopped. She turned to me and offered her lips. We kissed long and hard.

"I had a nice time, Charles," she said.

"I did too."

She turned and started to unlock her door. Before she went inside, she turned and waved.

"I will call you," I said.

"Thank you," she replied.

The door shut, and I stood there for a little while thinking about the kiss. It was so nice. I was hoping there would be many more. I knew, at this moment, I was falling in love with Debbie. It was not the first time I thought this. I couldn't wait to see her again.

The walk back to my apartment took about twenty minutes. I enjoyed the walk. It was rare that it would be such a beautiful night in San Francisco. Usually, there would be a cold wind from the bay blowing in. A chill would fill the air and you would have to bundle up with a warm sweater or coat, but not tonight.

Soon I was back in the apartment and was tired but upbeat. My mind was still reeling from the kiss with Debbie. I began going over in my mind our discussion about Todd. I again began to ache for Debbie. It was at this particular time my mind started to swirl.

I started to mesh things up in my mind. There was a whirlwind of thoughts coming to me. The finality of it all was perplexing to say the least. The uncertainty of life, as it unfolds before our eyes. Never knowing when it will cease. Perhaps we will all become extinct, like the dinosaurs of an ageless past. The philosophical and religiosity of existence become moot ideas of remembrance. Why are we here? To recreate the species and to love and be loved or perhaps, to find a friend who understands you. The golden egg of life reaching out to you becomes the mantra of life-form. The fountain of youth, which we all intuitively search for, becomes nothing but a figment of our imagination. The pervasive bent of the humans, who are seeking understanding, which may never happen.

We all want a deeper understanding of ourselves. Never achieving the nirvana we call the life-form. The carrot keeps pulling us away into the abyss of another tomorrow. Always the searching continues. The dawn keeps showing through, and the glorious sunsets on the open plains keep enveloping our souls. The breath of life keeps sucking in the planet Earth. One planet, among many, creating the greatest of wonderments, is a fact among facts. As Carl Sagan would say, there are literally billions and billions of objects in the universe and our planet is but a speck in the scheme of things. The life-form we seek in other worlds may be a dream too far.

Perhaps we are alone in the universe. Our insatiable quest for a deeper understanding of it all is compelling. The force of gravity which acts as one of the forces keeping us separated from the unknown. The black hole waiting for us to enter, just on the other side of realization, is an idea we can't ignore. The curvature of space-time is pulling us forward for all to see. It is there, as Einstein predicted. *How long do we wait for all the realities to come to the front?* I wondered.

The thought of Debbie talking to me about Todd was a little odd. What would cause me to come up with these ideas about the universal wonderments, because of the discussion about her friend Todd, I mused.

I began thinking more about our conversation at Saul's. Did Debbie know anything about my case from discussions with Dr. Law? I was on the fence about my approach to Debbie. With her studies in psychology, I needed to keep our first conversations on an even keel, at least until we became better acquainted. I did tell her about my early life to some extent. The conversation we had consisted of short bursts, as we were looking around at the people and listening to the DJ playing his records. He was entertaining to say the least and the music he was playing was not out of bounds, sound-wise.

I told Debbie that I was from Dent, North Dakota. That it was a small farming town in the middle of nowhere. I did tell her about my father, who was an alcoholic. For some reason, I got the sense she somehow knew I had a hard time while growing up. It was, however, conjecture on my part that she knew this.

All of the hurt came cascading down on me. My mother was a wonderful woman, who for some reason married a man of violent nature. Jeff Reed had quick flare-ups and violent mood swings which could become physical at times. My mother and I would always be on guard. He was a solitary man, as I discussed with Dr. Law. He drank heavily on the weekends but would never drink that much during the week. He was a good provider, and I often wondered if his drinking had to do with the pressure of making a farm run smoothly. On reflection, it did occur to me about a man taking on responsibility in life. Perhaps he really did not like farming. Maybe he was someone else entirely.

There was something about Jeff Reed that kept gnawing at me. Even at an early age, I had misgivings about him. This feeling would not go away. You think you know something, when in fact, you do not know the truth. I suppose we are all unique about these understandings about our parents. How deep do you go in trying to understand the personality of your father or mother? Can you actually absolve your feelings about them after they are no longer with us?

I felt more comfortable with my mother, even though she withheld the information about John. John Alexander was still on my mind. Everything that happened before had to be reconciled with this new revelation. The fact that my mother should have told me sooner about John played over in my mind many times and was a feeling I had to resolve.

Perhaps my interest in psychology was a way to understand what happened between Jeff Reed and me. There was so much I did not know about him. He was quiet most of the time. As a small boy, it was hard to get to know him. Sometimes he would just go off. I do recall times when he would explode for no apparent reason. There was nothing I did or anything my mother did that had any bearing on the outburst. We were obedient to his every whim. I did wonder at the time what caused his constant flare-ups. I surmised he was not happy and I think, in my mind, I considered myself responsible for this. In fact, I had the sense I was the cause of all the problems in our family. This became the guilt that was endemic in my personality. Of course I still remembered all the times my mother would tell me to lock the door. Now, I had Dr. Law, and to some extent, I had Debbie, to help me see the light.

The dreams I had as a child were clear evidence that I had problems. Reading Freud at a later stage in my life convinced me something was wrong. Lou tried to tell me years ago, but I was not open to seeking help. I knew, as time went by, that I needed help in understanding not just myself, but also the world around me. The shyness and uncertainty of the future was playing havoc with me. I wanted to be happy and enjoy life to the fullest. The evening was over, and now I wanted to sleep. MORE ON LOVE will continue in due course. I could hardly wait.

CHAPTER 7

*D*r. Law greeted me as I entered her office.

"Hi," I said, as I settled down in the chair.

"How are you?" Dr. Law asked.

"I guess I am doing all right."

She waited for me to start the session. Sometimes, it was hard to figure out how to begin. What I should discuss with her was always something that had to be faced. Since a lot of my early time with Dr. Law was concerned with my early childhood and the relationship with my parents, I now seemed to need a new exploration of my thinking process. Much of the guilt I felt for so many years about the family relationship was subsiding. But then the guilt would flare up, and I would again feel the angst of the time gone by. At the moment, I was thinking about Debbie, and I wondered if I should explore this burgeoning relationship with Dr. Law. Perhaps she could give me some insight into Debbie. After all, she knew Debbie pretty well, I reasoned. I decided that now was not the time for that discussion.

My job situation was another area that was bothering me. I was not satisfied with my position or the progress I was making. Maybe the dissatisfaction with my job was masking a different set of issues. Sometimes my emotional state was all jumbled together, like a ball of yarn. The unraveling was happening. I could feel it.

"I think I need a new job," I said.

"What is going on?"

I told her I felt like I wanted to do something different. I needed to do more exciting things with my life. She looked at me with interest. The conversation was different this time. I started to think more about my future rather than dwelling on the past. In my mind, this was progress. There was no need to rehash the past over and over. The abuse I suffered as a child was fading as a dark memory. The abyss of swirling thoughts and disconnected emotions became the forgotten ideas of long ago. Keep in mind, I knew that what happened to me would always be there, but I could better understand all the ramifications of the events. It was this therapeutic process that helped me see the light.

"What would you like to do?" she asked.

"I don't know, just something different."

She sat there in her usual stoic position. She waited for me to talk more. I had no idea what to say about what I wanted to do. I really could not describe what I was feeling. I just knew that I was not happy with my job. That was the bottom line. Helping clients with investments seemed like a worthwhile endeavor but it was not giving me the satisfaction I wanted. There was something missing. I had to explore different avenues.

"What are you thinking?" Dr. Law asked.

"Just trying to come up with a solution to this job thing," I said.

There were new ideas coming into the market. The internet and smart phone technology were exploding. I always had been interested in science, even though I majored in economics and philosophy. I did take some science courses as well. These disciplines seem to have empowered me to think differently. I could see how interrelationships about worldview fit together. It was, however, a conundrum for me to come up with solutions that I knew needed to be addressed.

I also had this notion of grief about the inequities that were inherent in our social system. Segregation, which permeated our society, was another idea I thought about a lot. It was good to start thinking about these different areas in which I seemed interested. How to proceed and make something different into a viable reality would take a lot of work on my part. It was something I had to solve on my own. Dr. Law could be a sounding board but the heavy lifting rested on my shoulders.

"Your time is up," Dr. Law said.

"So fast," I said.

I did feel better after this particular session. It started me thinking more about my future. I was unburdened by my past. Perhaps I was merely repressing these past emotions, and they would emerge another day. For now at least, I felt free to explore other ideas. Ideas that could help me become a happier person.

It was Friday, and I was thinking about Debbie. I kept going over in my mind our first kiss. It made me weak and wobbly. Soon I was in bed.

My thinking process continued searching for answers. Therapy did this to me. It made me think about all kinds of ideas. I began thinking about the learning process. If we can't learn, then we can't grow. I recalled reading about the how the brain works. The communication being delivered from one part of the brain to the other through the synaptic process was important in understanding learning processes in general. It appears that learning happens when the firing of these trillions of synaptic events happen in a coordinated fashion. The more direct communication these synapses have with each other, the more the learning process takes hold. Repetition is the soul of learning. At least, this is the way I understood it.

Soon I was sleeping. My Friday session was over and, as usually happened, it made me think about a variety of things. The unconscious mind started to take hold and the dreaming process began.

This dream unfolded as follows:

I was driving down a long narrow road. Off to my right side was a small town. Just before entering the town, there was a green lawn with large boulders strewn around. There was a hand motioning me forward. I kept driving toward the town. I kept getting closer and closer but the closer I got, the town started to change. Suddenly I was inside a large city with skyscrapers and cars going all around me. I became lost. Everything was unfamiliar to me. I became frightened. I wanted to call Debbie but my phone didn't work.

I woke up. It was three o'clock in the morning and I felt lonely, always alone. It was a manifest dream.

It was the following Friday and I thought I should discuss the dream I had last week with Dr. Law.

"Dr. Law will see you now," Joan said.

I had been sitting outside her office for awhile and I was wondering what I should talk about with her. After the dream I had the week before, I was wondering if I should talk about it. At the time after I had the dream, I thought I should talk to her about it but I hadn't yet decided.

I tried to formulate a discussion that would help me. It is not easy sometimes. *Should I talk about the dream or perhaps Debbie*, I wondered. I decided that my relationship with Debbie was something I didn't want to talk about at this time. I decided on talking to her about the dream. She sat there listening to me. She always had the same posture and expression on her face. After I finished telling her about the dream, she interpreted the dream as follows:

She indicated that the driving could represent a moving forward in my life. The greenness in my dream could be a need to grow more. The convergence of going from a small town into a large city could be another growth function. Although I said I wasn't going to discuss Debbie, it did come out in the dream. She said the fact I couldn't reach Debbie on the phone was probably because I was feeling unsure about the relationship. The fact I was lost in the big city was probably because it was a new experience and that I had to find my way. Growth is not easy, she said. Growing and evolving as a person can be painful. Sometimes you have to take a chance and see where you end up.

I thought about what she said and it did seem plausible. Trying to analyze dreams is difficult at best. In my mind, I had to see if what Dr. Law said fit with my understanding of myself. Should I take this as the gospel of what was really happening in my unconscious mind? How should I digest this and incorporate it into true understanding, as it related to my problems?

One of the things Dr. Law said to me was that she was trying to bring the multiple forces acting on my personality into one person. I started to become much more aware of what she was saying about this oneness idea. It did seem I was constantly being pulled in many directions. I could see being able to focus on one thing at a time could be powerful.

I became convinced that Dr. Law was on the right track. I wondered if she would say anything about Debbie during this session but she didn't. The need to continue in therapy was exemplified by the fact I could not forgive Jeff Reed and the way he treated me. It remained a memory which would not leave me.

In my mind, it was obvious the neurons and dendrites were circumvented from performing their proper functions. My brain's synaptic structure had been misfiring. The chemical process of neuronal development had been damaged by the horrific emotional trauma I suffered in Dent. Would I ever understand Jeff Reed's actions? The knowledge that he was not my biological father seemed to mitigate some of the feelings I had about him. The grotesque nature of all that happened was a fact I would have to bear. The events that happened to me in Dent were out of my control. In some way, I had to resolve this emotional chain that was smothering me. I was so inundated with the need to escape this wrath and unhappiness that my mind became transfixed with the abyss. The abyss in my dreams could haunt me forever in the dream state.

The eerie dreaming mind uncorked from reality and sent scurrying to Witches' Heaven. The emotional trauma was an unrelenting master, constantly picking and reminding me of the past. Wide awake forever would be the punishment. The gangsters and no-names were there for the taking. The constant pulling would not go away. This pulling was at the core of it all. *Am I or aren't I, the oneness of my own personality?* It was my hope that the splintered ego and id would become one. Hoping I could be free to see the light.

It was no wonder I would shake when I talked to Dr. Law about these early years. It was new to me to feel these emotions during my sessions. During this session, I seemed to regress some. Although I told Dr. Law I had forgiven Jeff, I couldn't help but remember the things that happened to me. I simply had to get it all out. The memories of the past would sometimes come crashing down on me. Unsuspecting and unannounced revelations would come in like the wave of a tsunami, uncontrolled and surprising.

Dr. Law was watching me. For some reason, I became uncomfortable. Everything went silent for a while as usual.

"What are you thinking about?" Dr. Law asked.

"Just thinking about Dent and what happened to me," I replied.

"What do you think?" she asked.

"I don't know. I guess I still feel guilty. I feel nervous."

"What do you feel guilty about?"

"I don't know."

I started feeling sweaty. I became focused on the fear that permeated my entire childhood. The heavy use of alcohol on the weekend was a big factor for his brutal behavior. I recalled what a solitary family we had. Our family had few friends. The friends we did have rarely came to our home. My mother and I would usually see them in church. The church was a good place to socialize. For my mother and me, it was the only place we felt safe. Church was a shelter in the storm for us. It was where many of the farmers around Dent would go to catch up on the news. Obviously, most of the news centered on the family and farming operations. Farming was a central theme discussed by most of the parishioners.

There is no doubt that North Dakota is a farming state. One could travel for miles and see nothing but fields of wheat and some corn crops. Most conversations would always end up talking about the weather. The weather, which impacts farming greatly, is often hard to predict and the farmers would get up bright and early and listen to WGOF, the weather station. Bill Mullen was the morning weather man. His program would start at four-thirty in the morning and last until nine.

Bill had been with the station for about ten years and all the farmers called him Billie. He had a smooth voice, and the farmers liked him. The information he espoused was important and the farmers listened to him with rapt attention. Bill would intersperse the weather with news about the county. Almost everyone would tune in to Bill at one time or another.

I kept thinking about Dent and about the farmers. Farmers are a hardy bunch. They would often work long hours in the oppressive heat to bring in their crop before the snow came. The usual climate in the Dakotas would consist of hot and humid summers interspersed with heavy rains and brutally cold winters.

Ours was a typical farm. In addition to growing wheat, we had five cows and three horses along with chickens and ten hogs. Each morning at four-thirty, I would get up and do chores. These chores would include feeding the animals and bringing in water from the outside well. I did these chores from as early as I could remember. Sometimes it would be snowing so hard, I could barely make out the barn from where our house was located. The distance from the house to the barn was only about 150 feet. Doing chores was something most sons who lived on a farm could not escape. I never resented doing chores but I did resent Jeff's attitude toward me. Jeff would always quiz me each morning about what I did. His attitude was always skeptical towards me, like he didn't trust me.

After I completed my chores, I would go back to the house and take a bath and get ready for breakfast. I remember it was always nice to get back to the house and smell the bacon and eggs my mother would be cooking. After breakfast, I would catch the bus, which stopped about a half mile from the house. It was nice when I was secure in my seat on the bus. Most of the time, I would sit with Irene and we would talk. The unhappiness of my situation was hard for me to grapple with at this time in my life. Words can't describe the horror. No laughter. Life was not the answer; it was the problem.

I told Dr. Law of my thought of suicide at a very early age. My mother would try to protect me from his abuse. His verbal thrashings and constantly putting me down was often more than I could bear. I wanted to leave but felt I should stay for my mother's sake.

"You are worthless, Charles. You will never amount to anything."

These were the comments I heard many times growing up under Jeff. I was always silent, as I was afraid of his wrath. He once hauled off and slapped me for no apparent reason. I became silent around him. I hate you, I thought.

"Jeff, how can you talk to your only son that way?" she asked.

"Keep out of this Beth and mind your own business," he said.

On this morning, I got my books from my room and walked out into the cold morning air. I was feeling unwanted and alone. *God, I wish I could die,* I thought. I wondered what he would do to my mother. I felt like I deserted her when I left. I loved my mother dearly. She gave me the strength to go on.

I was feeling very nervous talking to Dr. Law about these early years. She was showing understanding and compassion about what I was saying.

"You have come a long way," she said, after hearing my exhortations of my early childhood experiences.

This was the first time I had actually talked to anyone about these early experiences. Because of the constant abuse, my self-esteem had suffered greatly. The inferiority complex I developed was all-consuming. This malady became a force in shaping my personality. Social situations became unbearable. I would feel uncomfortable at the thought of interacting with others. I felt I was intelligent, but solving problems, either in my life or in the workplace, was difficult at best. It was like I would get so far and then self-doubt would creep in and usurp the answer. Trying to unravel these problems through the therapeutic process seemed overwhelming at best. The emotional strata of a dysfunctional personality would take years of tender prodding and exploration.

During this particular session, I thought about Debbie. I could never tell her the extent of my personal problems. The emotional tapes kept turning over in my mind.

The recurring memories were like waves crashing across the beaches in faraway lands. The need to exculpate the memory of my childhood was a goal I had to achieve. I must move on with my life.

The yoke of yesteryear is dragging me down.

The drowning despair must give way to a better tomorrow.

It was like a supernova had exploded in my brain.

CHAPTER 8

The death of Jeff filled me with sorrow and relief. He could no longer hurt me. My mother could now live a safer life. She stayed with him till the end. She endured his wrath and abuse for many years. Often when he would go hunting, my mother and I would play games. We used to cherish this time. It was a time we could both relax and enjoy the moment.

The front of the house had a view of the country road which passed by. There was a path which led from the house down the side of the road to a woody area where Jeff and other farmers around the area would hunt. As my mother described it to me, Jeff left to go hunting. It was something he had done many times. She said she watched him disappear around the corner of the path to the woods. Usually he would be gone for about three or four hours. He had now been gone longer than five hours.

CHAPTER 9

The heart is beating faster and faster until at last it beats no more. The crying soul of my memories has become one with the fowl, being eaten by the prey of the day. The reality has come full circle from birth to death. The smiling eyes above now have their respite. I am now in their arms. The tragedy has been circumscribed by a new progeny seeking new answers to the same old questions.

The explosion has happened.

The crunch has reached its course.

The shotgun mind has spewed the pellets of reversal.

I am now on a different arrow being propelled into a darkness of tomorrow.

An abyss steeped in misery everlasting. I have climaxed for the last time. I now cry for you my son, as the world now belongs to you. Don't be too critical of me until you know the truth. It will come to you in due course. I am sorry for what I did to you in my stupor. I know you never told anyone about this and I am grateful. I know one day this will fall upon you and you will cry inside. Goodbye for now.

I awoke and reality was before me.

This day was different and my mother sensed something was wrong. She decided to go search for him. She had walked about a mile through the bush calling his name. There was no response. He usually hunted squirrel and rabbit. He was a good shot and would often bring home several rabbits and squirrels for us to eat. He was a good provider in many ways. We never went hungry.

I was becoming nervous talking to Dr. Law about this. I felt myself becoming flush. I began sweating and feeling uncomfortable about it.

"How are you holding up?" she asked.

"It is something I need to talk about."

She was watching me intently. "Do want to continue this another time?"

I continued talking to Dr. Law about the event. As my mother further described it to me, she continued calling his name. No answer, only the call of a distant coyote. She continued walking. Finally, she saw a person from a distance sitting under a tree. She could not make out who it was. As she got closer, she could see it was Jeff. He was sitting there but crumpled over slightly and there was blood everywhere. She stood over him for some time wondering what to do next. He had committed suicide. She started crying. She sat down beside him for a while. The shotgun was by his side. The deed was done. The end had come. She rose up and started walking back to the house. The answer had arrived on a white horse to nowhere.

My mother called the sheriff and told him what had happened. She then called me and told me. I started to cry. Jeff was no more. His apology to me was conjured up in my mind. His asking for forgiveness was nothing more than a figment of my imagination. It became more of a need in me to find John Alexander. Maybe if I found him, I could achieve some comfort in my soul. Maybe the reconciliation of Jeff Reed could begin.

Although I had discussed the death of my father before, it still seemed to haunt me. I remember taking a philosophy course in college and the professor told us that sometimes you go around in circles, but each time you circle, new things could surface. Undiscovered ideas that were not there before was his central point. The death of Jeff was a circumstance which conjured up this philosophical idea.

After his death, I went back to Dent to be with my mother. When I arrived at the farm, the door was ajar and I walked inside.

"Mother," I yelled.

"Charles," she said.

"Yes, it's me."

"I am so glad you came."

We both walked back out onto the porch. There was a comfortable couch and chair where we could sit. I could tell my mother had been crying.

We started to talk. She said she called the sheriff and told him about the death. Ben Johnson, the Sheriff, knew Jeff as he had come in contact with him on one particular occasion. Jeff had gotten into a fight with his friend over a game of checkers. The friend called Ben to come and settle things down. Apparently, his friend accused Jeff of cheating.

It was Ben and the medics who went and retrieved the body. Dr. Wilson was Dent's only doctor and he was the one who made the determination that my father died by suicide.

As we were sitting there, I found myself tearing up. I didn't know what my mother would do now. I suppose I was also feeling sad about the death. Soon, tears ran down my face. My mother, too, started to cry. We both cried in silence. The uncertainty of the situation seemed dark. We would have to confront the reality of the present.

"What will you do now?"

"I will have to sell the house, as I am not in a position to take care of it alone," she replied.

"Can I help?"

"Just try to stay with me for a little while, if you can," she replied.

"No problem, I will call and take some time off."

I stayed two weeks. During this time, we found a buyer for the home. The buyer was a corporation and indicated they would probably change the configuration of the lease. The overall lease was on the farming acreage, which the corporation wanted to change. Their intention was to tear down the farm house and barn to make room for the planting of more wheat.

My mother decided to stay in Dent until she could recoup and do more thinking. She received 300,000 dollars for the home. Since the house was paid for, this would be enough for her to retire. She found an apartment around Dent. I stayed just long enough to get her settled.

The apartment she rented was small, one bedroom and one bath. There were four apartments in total. She had the top floor. She brought over some of the furniture from the house and furnished it quite nicely. The apartment was located just on the outskirts of Dent. She had a view of a creek, which ran just about 100 yards from her unit.

"Thank you, for coming and helping me," she said.

"No problem, but I need to get back to San Francisco."

"I understand," she said.

"I will keep in touch."

I walked over to her and gave her a long hug. "Goodbye, Mother."

"Goodbye, Charles."

We both cried. Jeff was gone. He could not hurt us anymore. We both expressed a deep sadness about it, though.

The ambivalence of the death and the relief was running through our souls. We had to carry on.

My flight back to the city was three and a half hours. Once airborne, I thought about Debbie. I did call her to tell her about being in Dent. I told her about the death of Jeff, but I didn't tell her that he committed suicide. *I'll tell her about his suicide at the right time,* I thought.

I needed to be alone with her. I wanted to love her. Make love to her was what I wanted right now. Thinking about Debbie at this time gave me solace from Jeff's tragic ending. There was nothing I could do now but think about Debbie and my future. The past about Jeff was gone.

During the flight back to San Francisco, I thought about how I could be alone with Debbie. I remembered that there was an off-ramp just off Highway 280. It led to a meadow that had a view of undulating hills and a few high-end homes that were tucked away far to the right of the meadow. This would be an ideal spot to take Debbie. You could see a long distance from the spot. There were small hills which mutated into a small mountain range. It was a tranquil setting for us to be alone.

As we approached the San Francisco airport, I looked down and could see the city shining below in all its glory. It was sparkling and beaming with life. I could see the cars going down Highway 280. It was good to be home. I took a deep breath and thought about Debbie again. I could hardly wait to call her. For some reason, the fact that Jeff was gone gave me a sense of relief. The ambivalence of the moment created the urgency to be with Debbie.

CHAPTER 10

I was tired of going over the same themes with Dr. Law. I needed to explore other facets of my personality. I wanted to know more about the world. I wanted to travel. I just needed to move on. The idea of moving on was a pervasive theme for me now.

"Hello," was the response on the other end of the line.

"Hi Debbie, this is Charles."

I told her about Jeff's suicide. I didn't tell about all the events that surrounded it, but I would tell her another time.

"Oh Charles, I am so sorry for your loss."

"Thank you."

I wanted to get right to the point about what I had been thinking about on the plane.

"I was wondering if we could take a drive tomorrow," I asked. "I really need to unwind from what happened."

"Sure, what time?"

"I thought we could rent a car and drive down to San Jose and then drive back up the El Camino Real and then back to the city."

"That sounds great. I will see you tomorrow then."

"Great, I will see you tomorrow."

After the call, I was euphoric. I was so relieved that she would do this.

I went over what I would talk to Dr. Law about. With the way I was now, maybe I should stop seeing her for a while. Let things settle and see how things go with Debbie and also make sure my mother was doing well. The constant regurgitation of themes over and over in my discussions with Dr. Law seemed so unproductive to me. I found it difficult to let go of the past. It was almost like an addiction. I just did not know what else I needed to do to rectify this. *I will decide about seeing Dr. Law later*, I thought. *For now, I just want to be with Debbie.*

I had the car delivered to my apartment. I rented it for one day. It was a midsize car, blue in color. The drive to Debbie's flat took just a few minutes.

When I knocked on her door, I was a little nervous. I was curious how my plan would work out. When she opened the door, she looked so beautiful. She had her hair down, and her makeup made her look even more beautiful. She was wearing a loose green dress, but you could still see the contours of her body. I got hard.

"Hi, Charles," she said.

"Are you ready?"

"I sure am," she replied.

It was a lovely morning. The sun was shining and it was cloudless. The wind was gently blowing in from the ocean. The temperature in the city was a nice sixty-seven degrees, just right for a nice drive, I thought. The drive to the San Jose area took about an hour.

San Jose is a large metropolis with a million people. I had been there several times and was always in awe of its growth. It seemed as though it sprung up all at once. It is the heart of Silicon Valley.

The trip down Highway 280 with Debbie was delightful. We talked about all sorts of topics. Mostly though, she talked about herself and her early years. She was also an only child. She loved both her parents dearly. She grew up in Muncie, Indiana. Her father became successful doctor in Muncie. They lived in a beautiful home on the outskirts of town. She said that Muncie was the center of a sociological study for many groups trying to understand middle class norms. Muncie had been designated as the ideal middle class community. Getting the mood of the country through the study of Muncie was an ongoing theme in the sixties and seventies. The town had a population of about sixty-five thousand when she lived there.

Her home in Muncie had three bedrooms and two baths. Her bedroom was quite large with a bath outside her room. She decorated it with various posters and art work. Outside the house was a large manicured lawn, which covered almost a half acre. It was a lovely lawn and was well maintained throughout the year, even in the winter months. There were flowers around the house, which Debbie liked to keep up. The house itself was of Tudor design. It was a brick house, as were many of the houses in Muncie. When winter came, the gardener would clear the area for replanting.

She also talked about the conversations they would have around the dinner table. They would look forward to these talks each evening. She was sure the conversations shaped her thinking and instilled a sense of comfort for her. The talks were an admixture of politics of the day to ideas about religion and other topics which were germane at the time. Although her father was a doctor, he was interested in psychology and so this was discussed from time to time. These talks happened when she was very young and, for the most part, she would just listen. The family was religious, but not overly so. They did go to church on most Sundays.

She seemed relaxed on the drive. She was talking a lot

more than when we would meet at Saul's. I loved listening to her talk. It seemed she talked about herself more and it was gratifying to hear her talk. I also started feeling she was more of a loner like me. *Perhaps that is something we have in common,* I thought. During the drive, there were moments when there was silence. It was a comfortable silence. Both of us were processing the moment.

I became hesitant to say too much about myself. I wasn't proud of my family background and I certainly could not compete with her upbringing. There was a fairly deep chasm that had to somehow be bridged. I wondered if it were possible.

I thought about my last session with Dr. Law. The idea of moving beyond my past was pushed back, as I could start to feel the rage in me bubble up. Could I burden Debbie with my problems? *Maybe I should not pursue her,* I thought. *Why was this rage happening? What was the reason I was starting to regress at this point in time?* I was with Debbie and it was such a wonderful day.

"Charles," Dr. Law said.

"Yes."

"Our time is up," she said.

"I have more to say."

"Next time," she replied.

As I rose from my chair, I felt uneasy. She gave me a faint smile as I left her office.

Why I would think about this session on the beautiful ride with Debbie was a bit of a mystery. Perhaps I was starting to confront my problems. It is odd how the mind works. How one's emotions can be recalled under certain circumstances.

After this session, I felt kind of liberated. Talking about the early years and reconciling issues which were presented to me offered a new perspective about how far I had to go. I was curious about the world. I thought maybe I was limited because of the circumstances that enveloped me in Dent. Now my life was being transformed by these sessions, and it started to stir in me the need to continue. It is like an addiction; the more I started to understand, the more I wanted to explore. A new curiosity was emerging and I was willing to go along for the ride. Just maybe, my stunted personality was on the move. Maybe, I was about to venture outside the cave. It was a good feeling and I wanted it to last.

I speculated about Debbie and the kind of life she had. The nurturing by her parents at a very young age was something I cherished. Her life and my life were different, but I was not so sure this difference represented something that we could not overcome. It was my thinking that nurturing was important. It was not Debbie's fault that I had the kind of life I had. I have tried to forgive the things that happened to me, but I have not reached that emotional plane yet.

San Jose was now coming into view. Debbie had been quiet for a while.

"How are you doing?" I asked.

"Just taking in the scene," she said.

She seemed like she was enjoying the trip. I drove into downtown San Jose. The skyline had been truly transformed. San Jose had gone from a small farming community to a metropolis.

"I have watched it grow for a number of years," I said.

CHAPTER 11

$\mathcal{A}$ s we were driving back, I asked Debbie if it would be comfortable if we could take the off-ramp in a few miles and take in the view. She said she didn't mind. I had actually taken the off-ramp once before and I thought it had a pretty view. You could see for miles. I parked the car and we sat there for a while, taking in the view.

"Would you like to get out and walk around?" I asked.

"Sure."

Very few people came here. There were some trees just down the dirt road which offered a lot of privacy. I opened the trunk and took out the blanket I had brought. We walked toward the trees. You could still see the view through the trees, but there was still privacy. I laid the blanket down below one of the trees and sat down. Debbie joined me. So far, my plan was working.

"This is so nice, Charles," she said.

"I know, I love it here," I said.

I had the sensation of closeness to Debbie. I decided to lie down. After a short time, Debbie joined me. It was like we were in tune with each other. She lay there face-up. I could not resist the temptation of the moment. I reached over and pulled her to me. We kissed. She put her hands around my head and pulled me closer. She wanted me as well. It was there that we made love. It was over so fast. It was exhilarating and it filled me with a wonderment I had never experienced. I wanted to be with Debbie so much longer. It could not have been better. We both enjoyed the moment.

The drive back to San Francisco was pleasant. Debbie seemed much more relaxed. I felt as though we were becoming friends and lovers. This was the kind of feeling we all want to have. During the drive back, I reached over and took Debbie's hand and put it on my leg. I wanted her again. She smiled as we continued the journey back to the city. I was surprised at myself for this action. It was so involuntary and natural.

When we arrived back to Debbie's flat, I got out of the car and we both walked to her front door. I said I'd had a great time. She said she had too. I looked around to see if anyone was around. Feeling comfortable, I took Debbie in my arms and kissed her. She responded by getting closer to me.

"Are you up to Saul's next Friday?" I asked.

"Sure."

"What time?"

"Well, I get off work at 5 PM so why not make it for 8 PM," she replied.

"Great."

"I will see you then."

It had been a fantastic day for me, and I was feeling happy. When I finally arrived at my apartment, I suddenly became tired. I decided to take a shower and relax. The shower felt especially soothing at this particular time. I turned the hot water up so that I could get the full impact and serenity of the moment. As the hot water swamped my body, I thought of Debbie. The whole sequence came crashing upon me. The lovemaking, as well as the breathtaking view from the trees, would forever be a memory I would cherish. The time with Debbie was glorious. I had a good feeling when I finally went to bed.

It wasn't long before I was fast asleep. Soon the dream state took hold. I found myself succumbing to the unconscious mind; the mysterious place we all try to understand but seldom do.

The dream unfolded:

I was walking into the woods. Tall trees with flowering plants permeated the scene. Before me was a lake. It was imbued with crystal clear, blue-green water. I found myself in a canoe paddling toward the center of the lake. When I looked down into the lake, I saw flickering lights. Soon there was a deep, open space and meteors were falling toward me. It was like I had entered a new galaxy. The event frightened me. I was lost and alone. I became disoriented and sweaty. The loneliness in my dreams seemed to be all pervasive.

Abruptly, I woke up. The time was 2 AM. The lake dream would come again at another time. Perhaps this was an important dream. I tried to understand the dream on my own. My thinking about the dream was as follows:

The trees were there because I was in the trees the day before with Debbie. The clear, blue-green water might be from my childhood in Dent. There was a small lake where I would go ice skating in the winter. Sometimes when the sun shone on the lake, there would be a bright glow and, in rare instances, a kind of rainbow would emanate from its surface. I always had fun ice skating there. Perhaps the dream was also telling me that not all my time in Dent was unhappy. The transformation of the lake into a galaxy could mean I was beginning to expand my thinking processes. The dual events of therapy and meeting and being with Debbie could mean I was starting to feel free within myself.

Maybe Dr. Law could shed more light on this. I even thought about asking Debbie for an interpretation but decided against it. She was my lover not my therapist.

She looked especially fetching the next Friday at Saul's. She wore a white blouse with a Levi's jacket with matching Levi's jeans. Her hair was down, just like it was when we went to San Jose. The experience of our lovemaking came crashing over me. I again became hard just looking at her.

"What is on your mind?" she asked.

"Oh, nothing," I lied.

Debbie and I needed to have more conversations. We needed to get to know each other better.

"I know this is off the wall, but what do you think about dreams?" I asked.

"Where did this come from?" she asked.

"I had a bizarre dream last night," I replied.

"Dreams are complicated and, from an analyst's perspective, you need to know the person quite well before you can attempt any credible interpretation of a dream," she said.

"Can you analyze your own dreams?" I asked.

"I suppose anything is possible, but it is always better to have a trained analyst decipher dreams."

I thought I would just start talking about something. We both needed to know how compatible we were. I thought we were compatible sexually, at least since we had been making love.

"What do you think about abortion?" I asked.

She looked at me for a little while before she replied.

"I am against it, unless the mother is in danger from the birthing process," she replied.

"That makes sense. Of course, there are other issues at play here. What about teenagers and unwanted pregnancies and incest, just to name a few of the issues that come into play?" I said.

"I see what you mean," she replied.

I could tell this was making her feel uncomfortable. She was moving around in her seat and started looking around at the crowd that was starting to develop at Saul's.

"I was just trying to make conversation," I said.

"I know, the abortion issue can be so divisive," she said.

"Yes, I know. I also think religions play a part as well."

"Pretty sure it does," she replied.

"The abortion issue merges in with overpopulation in my mind," I said.

"How so?" she asked.

"I think that each couple should be limited to no more than two children," I said.

"That would be hard to enforce."

I decided to press on with it in spite of her squirming. She had to know my views on this. "Something has to be done about overpopulation; it will eventually destroy the planet. If you believe Thomas Malthus, the food supply will eventually become deficient in feeding the world's population. Already 821 million people go hungry each day. In my mind, this is unacceptable," I said.

"Thomas Malthus?

"He was an English economist who studied demography. He is the one who came up with this theory about the food supply running out due to overpopulation," I said.

I continued talking to her about this.

"It is not just the lack of food situation it is also the overall crowding of our cities and roads. The overpopulation creates a myriad of other problems, such as pollution and the stress which affects us all. In my mind, it does create a kind of doomsday scenario. All these problems become insurmountable. The planet is suffering and we are at a loss to find a solution."

"You seem pretty pessimistic about this," she said.

"Do you see any hope?" I asked.

"I really haven't given it much thought."

She might construe from this conversation that I didn't want a family. The conundrum about having a family, and also not wanting to overpopulate the planet, was a stressor for me.

"That is the point I am making — not enough people are giving it enough thought," I said. "Climate change is the other part of the equation. It is coming fast and I do not see enough being done to protect the planet, especially as it relates to the young people. It is really mind-boggling that we let this happen."

"You seem a little upset tonight," she said.

"I guess I am."

"Do you want to talk to me about it?" she asked.

"Sometimes I get a cloud over me."

"What do you mean?" she asked.

"Maybe we will talk about it sometime."

She sat back in her chair and looked at me with a steady stare. It was like she was trying to analyze me. I became a bit antsy, and I guess it showed, as I took a big gulp of wine, something I rarely do.

The crowd at Saul's was getting pretty loud as the acoustics seemed to be failing.

"Would you like to go?" I asked.

"Sure."

We took the usual walk to her flat. It was a nice walk. When we arrived, she asked me if I wanted to come in.

Her flat was nicely decorated. There was one large living room and a large kitchen with modern appliances. The living room consisted of a three-person sofa and two matching swivel sofa chairs. The white furniture sat on a thick Berber rug which offered a very inviting aura. There were three pictures in the room. One of the pictures was a skyline of New York City. Another picture looked like something Dali would have painted. It was of a warped piano, purple and blue in color. The other picture was similar to the artwork in Dr. Law's office. It was a picture of squiggly green lines mixed with warped circles going every which way.

"Would you like a glass of wine?" she asked.

"No, but I would like some ice water, if you have any."

Under the picture of the warped piano, there was a gas fireplace and above the fireplace and just below the painting was a mantle with a few pictures on it. One picture was of two people, a man and a woman. My guess was this must have been her parents. The other picture was of a single male. He had a good physique and was wearing a ski jacket and a black ski hat. That must be Todd, I supposed. On the other side of the room was a flat screen TV and below that was a stereo system which seemed connected to a central sound system. Very nice, I thought.

"Here you go, Charles." She handed me the ice water.

"Shaved ice, I love shaved ice," I said.

"Yes, I do too," she replied.

"I am going to change into something more comfortable, if you don't mind," she said.

"Oh, no problem," I said.

Before she went to change, she turned on the sound system, and the music was light classical. It was a piano concerto which, if I were to guess, was Brahms. She also started the gas fireplace and then turned the lights down. *Hmm, I wonder if she is trying to seduce me,* I thought. I was hoping that was the case. It was so relaxing being with Debbie. The music and the glowing fire created a sense of belonging. It was surreal in many ways, but importantly, I had never felt that in my life.

When I first came in, I sat down in one of the sofa chairs,

but when she left to change, I decided to move over to the three-person sofa. It was more comfortable.

"Are you comfy, Charles?" she called out from her bedroom.

"I am fine. Take your time. I am enjoying the fire and music," I replied.

"That's nice."

I laid my head back and closed my eyes. I was a little giddy from the wine I had at Saul's. Debbie took about ten minutes to change. I was picturing what she might be wearing when she came back. I was hoping it would be something loose-fitting. I didn't want to struggle, I mused. My feeling at that moment was that I thought Debbie wanted to make love as well.

"I am back," she said as she entered the room.

"You look gorgeous," I blurted out.

She emerged wearing a loose two-piece red silk lounging outfit. She had her hair down like it was when we made love coming back from San Jose. She went over to the sound system and changed the record. She put on an oldie by Dean Martin called "Return to Me."

"So enticing" I said.

"Yes."

She came over and sat next to me. We sat there for a little while listening to the song. She then decided to put on a CD of various songs. The music was romantic music from the fifties. She moved closer to me. Soon I took her in my arms. We kissed for quite some time. We were enjoying each other. Soon we were on the rug and I removed the bottom part of her outfit. I slowly started massaging her body. I began kissing her. She became aroused, and our lovemaking ensued. I tried to stay inside her for as long as I could. I didn't want to leave her. We climaxed together. We both laid there for a while. A feeling of contentment ruled the moment.

"Do you want to take a shower?" she asked.

"I would love to."

Soon the warm water was falling over us. I again took her in my arms and caressed her. After the shower, I got dressed with the sense that I had just experienced heaven.

For some reason, John Alexander came into my head. I had not told her about John Alexander yet. I just wanted to get to know her better. I would tell her in due course, though. I somehow felt if she knew this fact of my life, that she would think less of me. The blueprint of my life was so jumbled and mixed up. I needed to talk with Dr. Law about this. The conversation at Saul's was a little much. I found myself getting carried away about things. I just needed to cut back and relax. She was intelligent, and I needed to find out more about her views.

The dream I had the night before was relevant.

It unfolded as follows:

It was snowing and cold. I was in my room. The lights were out. There was a loud banging on my door. Open the door! I was frightened. Lock the door, Charles! Open the door! Back and forth it went. The window to my room was cracked open. I jumped out of it and into the cold night. I started trudging through the snow. I had no idea where I was going. I felt so alone, so terribly alone. I was friendless. I needed help but no one was there. I vomited from the anxiety.

I woke up.

Unlike before, whenever I had a dream. I would just try to understand it to the best of my ability. This dream was different because it reflected a throwback to my past in Dent. I etched this dream into my memory. I deemed this my "Snow Dream" because I needed to remember it and try to solve the meaning of it going forward.

How does one recoup the damage that was done to one's soul? Going forward in life, we all want to be happy. The happiness we seek is wrapped up in our emotional well-being. We must try to root out the devil of emotional trauma and exculpate the feelings that these various traumas engender. The guilt that was thrust upon me at a young age was what I was dealing with now. The resolution was to get a good understanding of my situation at the time of my youth. I was trying, through the therapeutic process, to unwind all the events which were causing these guilty feelings, and thus, were preventing me from being happy. It wasn't just my dreams, but also my behavior and how I would respond to things which led to my unhappiness.

I recall Dr. Law would ask me how I would behave in certain situations. She wanted to see how I reacted to events that were happening in my life. I remember a situation happened on my job. My supervisor, Doug, asked me if I had a report ready. I said I had not finished the report as yet. He pressed me further about it, and I blew up at him. It was not a good sight to witness. Others around my work area were taken aback. Doug immediately told me to come to his office. He told me if that ever happened again, that it would be cause for dismissal. I told him I was sorry. When I told Dr. Law about the event she said that was not something that was unexpected, given what I had been through. My behavior was out of bounds and almost cost me my job. I had a lot of anger inside me that needed to come out. It had to be managed and delivered in a responsible way. This was not the first time my anger had got the best of me. So many people do not have the luxury of therapy, I thought.

"I must go now," I said.

"You can stay here for the night," she replied.

"That is nice of you, but I have some things I must do."

"I understand. I had a nice time," she said.

"Yes, me too," I said.

I walked over and took her in my arms and caressed her.

We kissed again, and I began getting aroused. This feeling was unbelievable to me. It wasn't long before we found ourselves in her bed. *So much for leaving tonight,* I thought. We made love again. Soon, we both fell asleep.

When I awoke the next morning, Debbie was still sleeping. I arose and got dressed, trying not to wake her. She was beautiful and was sleeping so peacefully. On the way out, I found a pad of paper and pencil and left her a note: "Debbie, I didn't want to wake you. I will text you later. Love, Charles".

The walk to my apartment was brisk. On the way, there was a park where I would go occasionally to relax and shoot some hoops. There was a basketball court and tennis court which were surrounded by a lush green rolling lawn. There were several benches. I decided to sit on one of them and relax before going home. I thought about the lovemaking with Debbie and how wonderful it was.

I thought about my friend, Lou, whom I had not seen in a year or so. I sent him a text: "Hey Lou, long time, no hear. We should get together. Let me know. Charles".

Sitting there, I also wondered about Irene. I wondered how she was doing in New York. *I will have to try and find her number.* I wanted to tell people about Debbie. Irene was one of my dear friends in high school. I also thought about Dr. Law. I pondered whether I should stop therapy now that I was with Debbie. The fleeting idea of stopping therapy was invalidated by my Snow Dream. *I must pay attention to this.*

I gradually began looking more toward the future. My goals were also changing. I wanted to have a home of my own and a nice car and other material things. I needed a road map. *Maybe Dr. Law can help me with this.*

CHAPTER 12

I remembered meeting a person at one of Joe Benson's parties. Joe was a friend of mine. I met Joe at Jake's in San Francisco. He had an import/export business and did quite well. Joe introduced me to Paul Cramer. Paul was a financial guy who had his own business. At the time, I thought Paul was a stand-up guy. He seemed knowledgeable about the financial arena. Although my first instinct was to call Joe, I could not find his number. I took a chance and decided to go and see Paul.

"So, I take it you are interested in making an investment of some kind," Paul said.

"I think so it just depends on how much I need to come up with."

"So, how much money can you come up with?" he asked. I was taken aback by this.

"I may have $5,000." I replied.

"Wow that is really a low amount. We usually ask for $50,000 as a starting investment."

I shrank in my chair. I knew I was not going to be able to

come up with that kind of money. We sat there for a while not talking. I felt flush. My hands were again becoming moist.

"Well, I appreciate your time, Paul, but there is no way I can come up with that much."

"Wait a minute. Let me make a phone call."

"Hello, Ron, this is Paul. Listen, I have a friend who wants to invest with us, but he does not have the necessary minimum we need. He says he has $5,000 that he can come up with. What say you?"

My assumption was that Paul had a partner he had to check with about the dollar amount. After the call, Paul looked at me with a smile on his face and said that they would do the deal for $5,000.

"Send us a check, and we will get started."

"Do you have any idea about how you will invest the money?"

"We will probably start off with a good diversified portfolio and see how it goes."

"Thanks, I really appreciate you doing this for me."

"No problem, we will be in touch."

I was starting to feel hopeful. It would not be easy to get the $5,000, and I still had to figure that out. I knew it was risky and costly to some extent, but I had faith in Paul and his company. I had a good feeling about Paul, just like when I first met him.

As soon as I left his office, I went to the bank, charged my card, wrote out the check that same day and mailed it to Paul's office. The deed was done.

After going over the various options I had available, I agreed with Paul that a diversified portfolio made the most sense. Paul told me that it was less risky but that we could see how it went.

CHAPTER 13

*R*egression is always a possibility, especially when you are trying to overcome the odds, the long odds of life. Life is foundational. If you do not have the proper grounding at a young age, it will be a struggle for most of your life, at least that was what I thought. Just when you think you have it all worked out, something triggers these dangling emotions inside. Perhaps, I thought, I was afraid of success. I was doing fairly well, but maybe my soul was rebelling.

For some reason, I thought about Plato and the allegory of the cave. It was a concept in philosophy that intrigued me when I was in college. It stuck with me and I would often reflect on the idea during some of my down moments.

The allegory was a hypothetical analysis of prisoners being chained at the bottom of a cave. There was light being reflected against the cave wall. The prisoners believed the images they were seeing were real. Some of the prisoners broke free and ventured up further in the cave and found that a fire was projecting the images on the cave wall. They knew then that the images were not real but reflections from the fire. They had found the truth. The truth is sometimes hard to grasp. When the prisoners tried to go back into the cave to free the other prisoners, they became blinded by the darkness. Knowledge and perseverance were the hallmarks of true leadership. Those that made it out of the cave into the sunlight were the philosopher kings. It took courage to reach into another realm, I thought.

I continued my sessions with Dr. Law. We continued delving into my psyche. The madness of my soul and tossing and turning of my essence seemed to counter any progress I thought I was making. The scattered remains of days past were being swallowed up by the ghosts of dying vats. These were the wormy, rotting vats aboard the ship of yesterday. The drunken brawls permeated the night. The red glow of a wino sacked out in front of a beaten down shack in the middle of nowhere. The shallow eyes going nowhere but down into the abyss of forgetfulness. The weight of the world shrunk down to the size of an atom. Compressed into the sinking hole of life for all to see, never challenged, not even once. Free floating space before our eyes.

Staring and gawking, more than a mere grasshopper, slinking like a snake with bulging eyes. The uncommon remorse at the plight of humanity sulking into the night of forgiveness, creating a false idea of happiness was a new thought that I was having.

The trees of the earth, seeking to escape the sickness of their roots becomes all pervasive.

The rulers of the past and present looking down their noses which had been stuck in the air, grinning out loud like the blast of bombs exploding with a vengeance. The trembling, shaking vomit of a drug addict, searching for his insides but finding nothing but blood in a graveyard of heroes searching for redemption of this troubled time.

The continuing drive to madness continues unabated. The black box of life regurgitating the sorrowful epitaphs of soldiers past and present not looking to the future but stuck amidst a time warp forevermore. The lock on nature by those who must reconcile the beginnings of the universe must try to stand tall and rebel. The wind is blowing in every direction which manifests itself, like the squiggly lines in the painting in Dr. Law's office.

The laws of man run rampant, like butterflies being smashed against the rocks on the shore of the Pacific. The meandering rivers of life filled with fossils of days gone by. Smiling dinosaurs wondering what has become of the planet since their departure. Asteroids exploding in the faraway world we call the void. Understanding of time as it marches to nowhere. Gentrification of the body, as the biological clock keeps ticking. Moving up and down the ray of light, seeking answers to the eventual death of us all.

The madness of thought of all things concrete, searching for the despots of the present and future who know of misery around them but only smile a smirking smile of greed gone haywire. The censors of the world who tell us what is supposed to be good for us, stamping us down like a beetle squashed on the highway of life. The constant searching for the true meaning of it all, as if that is what we are supposed to do. The dabbling into things unknown and reaching back to the familiar, afraid to continue. Afraid of what we might find. The resurrection of the Christ Child is something to behold, and seeing the realities of the moment searching for the perfect paradigm to ease the pain of continuing of life's struggle. These can be the best of times for those who can conquer the fears of the unknown. The priests of today trying to predict when the Nile will flood harkens back to the ones who know it all. The Vikings of yesterday masturbating their life away aboard the ships of fools going nowhere, was an idea that rang in my consciousness. I can see now the swirling fog moving into the harbor of life.

The same theme, repeated a thousand times over and over again, wearing a different mask. The fear of being different than the rest is the watchword of the future. What is the use of going on if you are on the way to nowhere, couched in the belief that things will get better. Money rules! Human nature remains the same, unchanged from the days of the beginning. Apes eating sour grapes and liking it, is the mantel they carry into the future. They are fooled into believing this is all they have. The rising head of us all beaten down a million times by the cagey ones who want it all for themselves. Sophisticated games being played by those who know the difference between the lower and higher truths of life are not for the faint of heart.

Always remember the philosopher kings of Plato's time searching for ways to enrich themselves in the understanding of human nature. We must obey the laws of the rich and powerful, being guarded by good lawyers who are all on the take. These shady people who will defend their rich clients to the last man standing, even if it means the end of us all. This is an urgent call for us all to heed, the end of our way of life could be just around the corner.

We must speak up now before it is too late, or we will sulk away into nothingness. The orchestration of this uprising can only come from the ones who know. The others are fools of the Nazi era who will not listen to reason but will confront you with inane ideas which are incomprehensible. Run my friend into another world of knowing. This will be your reward. The truth will set you free, as they say. You and I will hold hands together and confront this madness. The futility of a mind gone haywire is what I am now facing. The ethics of life is now in right field, along with all the people caught up in the madness of the times, striving to complete a moral compass we can all follow.

The shaking begins as I encounter the deeper core of my

essence. The wall of life is crumbling before me. Life is a day-by-day affair. A life filled with emotions of yesterday and the thoughts of tomorrow, a tomorrow which may never come.

Sweating continues as we explore the abuse of a childhood gone sour. Sour as green grapes the apes ate a million years ago. I can see them now, swinging from tree to tree, consuming the fruits of their labor. The evolution continues until we find ourselves no closer to the truth than in those days. The serene moonlit nights, with the carbon monoxide grabbing at our throats, choking us unconscious and unaware of what is happening. Kicking us down again and again until the night finally comes, and we can enter the dream state of forgiveness. Disorder abounds in a world seeking a higher king but only finding a mortal soul snacking on chips and salsa. The entrusted leaders schooled in the rich comfort of a fluffy chair in which I find myself. A couch chair in Dr. Law's office, not fluffy, but firm!

We all seek to escape the folly. Which course do you take? Ah, you see it can be predetermined. What was your childhood like? These are the questions. So much depends on your upbringing. What do you have to overcome? How you get from point A to point B is the overarching idea you must solve. To return to the womb in the swirling light of infinity is only a thought process grounded in the experience of days gone by. The rise and fall of the human spirit is a never-ending drama we must all confront. We must seek the right path.

The forgiveness of the father who raised me would have to wait another day. The seething hatred for him was all-consuming. It went deeper than I had suspected. The pounding heart of a frightened child on the prairie in North Dakota was my cross to bear. A good boy, only wanting to be left alone, but it was not to be. The precious family destroyed by a generation of strugglers with closed-down minds living off the land of someone else, with a sharecropper attitude seeking nothing but a rabbit and a good screw. Never understanding the electron volt and electrodynamics as it related to the scheme of things going forward was like a faraway dream.

The plowshare mentality in my father's mind, seeking nothing but revenge from a troubled past, which he brought to bear on our family. A crackerjack kid, beaten down by the land and the need to survive, was only the beginning of what I had to overcome. Failing in his attempts at fathering was not lost on my mother, who was always there for me. It was she who gave me the strength to carry on. We all need someone. The circumscribed moments when all seemed hopeless, my mother was there most of the time. I must still reconcile her hiding from me the truth about my real father. I must continue searching for my soul.

Debbie and Dr. Law and Lou, and also Irene, were so important for me in my early years. The SHOTGUN had fired and my father lay dead under a tree on a chilly morning in North Dakota.

"Our time is up," Dr. Law said.

Her face was firm and resolute. She showed some empathy for my discovery: the discovery that my father had a tougher time than he gave me was a first step in knowing the truth about my past and hence the future. This was not the first time I thought I had forgiven him. He was not to be hated, but rather pitied and forgiven. My understanding of him had changed since I found out about John Alexander. I will forgive him eventually, I suppose, but now was not the time.

It had been a month since I met with Paul. *I will call him tomorrow. Tonight, I will sleep alone with my thoughts. Debbie where are you?*

CHAPTER 14

*W*e are all encumbered by certain social stigmas from our beginnings. This social bias is foisted on us by our environment. To break out of the lower social strata is not easy. It requires brains and luck. It was no secret that my upbringing was not of the noble set. I would have to make it on my own.

I had been following my portfolio for a while now. It had increased in value. Actually, one of the stocks split and another was on the verge of buying out another company. I had been keeping track of this since I made the investment. When I called Paul, he was very excited.

"Why not sell now, and take your profit?" he asked.

Unbelievably, the portfolio had increased by $2,000 in a month. I thought it strange that he wanted me to sell after such a short time.

"I am onto an IPO that will be coming out in a few weeks. I have been following the company for a year or so. I think it would be a good investment."

"What kind of company is it?"

"It's a high-tech company working in the area of automotive engineering," he said.

"OK, let me think about it."

My job at First Financial was improving, especially since I was investing on my own. What happened next was unbelievable. I called Paul and told him to sell my shares in CAM Co. The digital option was not doing as well, so I told Paul to let it expire. The idea of being wealthy was starting to become a reality on a small scale. I could see, though, that things were starting to work out.

I did not tell Debbie of my investment activities, since I didn't want her to be upset with my wild speculations in the options market. In my mind, Debbie was pretty conservative, and if she knew what I was doing, investment-wise, it was my feeling it could be a deal-breaker in our relationship. I decided to withhold my various schemes until I knew her better.

Options are creepy and require constant oversight. I would check them constantly on my phone and computer. When I got off checking them on the phone, I called Paul.

"I want to buy 15,000 shares of Rico Inc."

"Charles, you have to be nuts to do this. Don't you know how risky that can be?"

"I know, but this is what I want to do. I have been following Rico for a while, and I got some good news about the company going forward."

Paul made the purchase that day. Now it was a waiting game.

After the conversation with Paul, I decided to take a walk. The weather outside was a little cool. Autumn was beginning to raise its head, as it always did. San Francisco is beautiful this time of year. I left the apartment around 3 PM. The city was alive and vibrant. The tourists had gone back to wherever they called home. The cable cars were not as crowded as in the summer. The walk from my apartment to the ocean would take about an hour or longer. I needed to go to the ocean. I needed to breathe in the salty air and reflect on my decision to buy Rico Inc. *I should tell Debbie.* I was starting to feel guilty about this. I would tell her soon enough.

The need to be by the ocean was a constant pull on me. I wanted to sit on the beach and watch the waves rushing toward me. Savoring this moment in my life was something I wanted to remember. For good or bad, it was just the memory of it that I wanted.

The sand was surprisingly warm from the sun's rays beating down through the day. The beach was beautiful. I looked out on the ocean and saw a freighter making its way to various destinations in the Pacific realm. Who were the people on board? The ship's hands had probably made the crossing many times. What kinds of things occupied the time on these long journeys?

I thought about Debbie. I imagined what would happen to us. Would we be married and have a family? Would we travel? Our lovemaking was so divine. I cherished it so. The thought of her with me made my head spin. Lying next to me and wanting me. Her breasts against my chest offered me the best memory I could have.

It was a wonder of life's plan and the full embodiment of the processes of life which were captured in the moment at this time. The full circle of life unfolding before our eyes and the penetration of the genes were all the thoughts I was having, as I dangled my feet in the cold water of the Pacific Ocean. The replication of the species and the grand plan unfolding in a beautiful fulfilling unabashed realm of the unknown was one of the translucent moments going forward. The lingering moments of orgasms were swirling around me and created a blanket to keep me warm — warm from my time with Debbie. The beauty of the ocean uncorked, like a genie in the bottle of life, floating through the cosmos. Does everything become uncorked in time?

The ocean brought out the best in me. It was so brutal and unrelenting, yet it had a calming effect. It was always in motion and endless; like the wind blowing through the outer reaches of the earth. MOVING UP and out like me, trying to overcome the impossible. I would keep growing, like the kelp in the ocean, always seeking the sun for nourishment.

I must have Debbie again. I was missing her now. Missing her tenderness and beauty, I could hardly wait to have her again. Pulling her to me was an act I cherished. The sweet explosion filled the air. The sun was fading into oblivion as I decided to make my way back home. The walk back was all uphill. I took a deep breath and started the trek.

CHAPTER 15

*I*t was a constant challenge to find things to discuss in therapy. There were times when I thought everything was OK, and then something would prick my consciousness and I would revert back to the beginning. The snow dream came to my mind, like a flash from the start. For some reason, I did not want to discuss the snow dream with Dr. Law. I was afraid she would think I was falling backwards in the process. Maybe, I thought, all things can't be reconciled. Often, I would just talk about whatever was on my mind. There were times when I felt the process was moving too slowly.

How long before I can achieve a final solution to my problems? During one session, I remember discussing a dream I had the night before. When I sat down, Dr. Law was staring at me. She seemed focused on me. OK, she was saying in a nonverbal way, what is on your mind today?

I recalled the dream as follows:

"I was being sucked into a black hole and my body was becoming elongated. I was clawing at it, trying to stop the free fall. There was enormous pressure on me from all sides."

"You mean you were clawing at thin air?" she asked.

"I guess so."

"How did the dream end?"

"I just woke up. I do remember sweating a lot."

"Feeling bad?" she asked.

"I felt lonely."

"How long have you felt this way?" she asked.

"Not too long."

"Did you have trouble going back to sleep?" she asked.

"Not really, it didn't take too long to go back to sleep."

She was looking at me in her usual way. Her posture was stoic. She was very alert. "What do you think the dream means?"

I moved around in the chair, thinking of what I could say about it. "It seemed as though I was falling. Like my life was still on a downturn. It seemed like my life was going down into this deep hole."

"Yes, but at least you were trying to catch yourself during the free fall," she said.

I thought about what she said, and I could see that the sessions were probably acting as the claws, trying to stop the free fall into the black hole in my life. I was indeed trying to turn things around. The black hole dream offered an insight into my psyche. I was starting to have some exciting moments in my life. I thought I would forget the snow dream as just an aberration. In my mind, it was a fluke in the overall scheme of things. I felt I had come so far, and then my dream pulled me back to the start. The cold snowy nights and days of my youth were again in front of me seeking an understanding of what happened. *The analysis will be forthcoming in due course,* I thought.

The lovemaking with Debbie was so nice and wonderful. The investment in Rico Inc was proving to be a good one. There were times when I thought about stopping therapy.

The black hole dream, however, convinced me that there was more to explore. There did seem to be a need to continue with therapy.

During one of the sessions several weeks after I had the black hole dream, I told Dr. Law that I felt everything was fine with me. When I said this, she looked at me with her penetrating eyes for quite some time but said nothing. When I got up to leave she said that she would see me next time. *I guess she will not be saying a final goodbye.*

There is something about feeling good. You have to be careful. Life can be funny, up one day and down the next. The Yin and Yang of the moment keeps repeating in a never-ending stream. Hopefully, the ups become more constant. Day by day, one has to become happier. The emotional whirlwind was not easy though, as my mind would not let me forget the past. The misery of the past keeps intruding in brief moments to let you know your place in the universe. Trying to overcome past traumas was proving to be exceedingly difficult. The therapy process was slow and I would often find myself in a state of nervous anxiety. The mania always seemed to creep in. The human tapes of days gone by keep playing over and over. Lucidity comes more frequently. The step by step building of the ego was being deftly handled by Dr. Law.

From infancy to old age, the process of trying to grow continues. If any links in the process of emotional growth are missed, then there will be gaps in the personality structure. There would be a lack of completion in the process. It is about the process. The unraveling of the mind is thrust forward into a new world; a world that is bright and fulfilling. The mind is so fragile and complex, I thought. It is a marvel that there are people who can understand the myriad complexities of it.

With the help of Dr. Law, perhaps I could resolve the issues that were preventing me from going further. Dr. Law was patient with me. She was always encouraging me to talk.

We seemed to have reached an accord on how the unraveling should proceed. Most of the communication was nonverbal. For example, if I found myself wandering from the main issue, she would look away as if to say, this not on point: let us stick to what is important to you. Sometimes, I would rage at the world and then I would become calm and serene. Sometimes, I would feel like a king. Perhaps a philosopher king, I mused. Often I would think thoughts which didn't seem to fit my personality. Lofty thoughts of the noble kind would protrude into my thinking processes, similar to a magic wand that was being waved over me. Then out of the blue, something would prick me like a thorn bush in North Dakota and bring me back to reality. The feeling good part was followed by shaking and a small degree of fear. The fear of success was something I had confronted often in my life. The cleansing of the past was sometimes more than I could bear. In my mind, I felt embarrassed by the revelations which were unfolding. I would even wonder if I could trust Dr. Law with these memories and traumas which were coming into clear focus. It could not be a pleasant sight to see someone shake with fear of what might be discovered. The shaking would always happen when I began to feel superior to others. The mystery would be solved someday, I hoped.

The throbbing heart echoing in my ears and the sleepless nights of tossing and turning were but some of the symptoms which I had to endure. Often, I found myself roaming through a maze of nothingness. The text was out of shape. The rambling verse of nonsense protruded in the shadows. The black hole dreams I had of a universe gone astray and the ever-present head of an ox always creeping in, just waiting for something positive to happen. The symbolism of the ox with the yoke around his neck was something to understand.

So goes the sing-song style of a mind searching for the key to unlock the morass of despair. I was afraid to go too far with the analysis, as I felt unready to confront the inevitable. I was unwilling to allocate time to solving the problems, which to me seemed couched in a never-never land.

My interest in things scientific would sometimes prick my senses. The deep shadowy problems that I was aware of in the scientific arena became visible from time to time. The concept of space and time warped in on itself. Proton decay and antigravity were just some of the unresolved notions which interested me. These were ideas which were beyond the scope of my mental makeup. I was afraid to proceed to try to solve issues related to these brave topics. I knew they existed, though. I was content to let others reap the glory.

The sweating continued as I cooled down into the reality of my existence. The juggernaut and misery of life was unfolding and creeping into the reality of the moment.

The pictures in Dr. Law's office seemed to have taken on a different meaning, as I now found myself recouping the loss of years gone by. Rather than seeing a swirling of nothing-ness, I began to see patterns of interconnecting events. The twelve apostles were there to behold. The Last Supper being eaten for all eternity stood out in stark contrast to what I was seeing before. The sea was opening up for me to enter. The invitation to enter was mailed RSVP.

My couch chair was getting tiresome, as I was seething into the nothingness of despair. The smiling head of life was recouping all its gains. I began giving back to the monster of my soul. The superior attitude was in shambles before my feet. The same constant theme told a thousand different ways.

The sun was starting to vanish, as the fog moved in under the Golden Gate Bridge. The substance of life, for a few moments in time, became nothing but a scant shadow of a time gone by. We need the sun to carry on the stuff of life for a few moments before we assume a role in the world. The role we are destined to play in the never-ending stream of consciousness. What are we really searching for but happiness? Elimination of fear is the catchword of the day.

The epistemology of the "Good," as espoused by G.E. Moore takes on a new meaning for me. The nub of it all seems to be contentment. Without this, we are forced to grovel in a pit of nothingness. No meaning, just a rambling, rolling period of existence. All the questions I have asked are opaque to me in so many ways. Does time go backwards or forward into the void? Is the microanalysis complete? Does time master all? When is the true end of time? Does the body rise from the ashes and become a tree? Has the cosmology been rectified by the arching light of stars as it passes the sun? Where are we going with all of this? Is this what constitutes the madness of my soul? Our soul! Do you believe in "It"?

The constant searching of the unknown looking for answers but not finding satisfaction. The event of electron annihilation as it becomes part and parcel of the zoo of elementary particles. The big bang on an epic scale infused in our thinking in the moment. When did time begin? Before the big bang, I wondered. Quarks of the proton to the nth power composed of quarks of tomorrow. Will there be decay of proton development? If they indeed decay, will the universe start to revert into the big crunch? The sparking of the trees as protons decay and the universe starts its decent into oblivion. Soon they will reach their endpoint. The never-ending stream of forgetfulness is still with us.

The annihilation of matter does some violence to the modern theory of physics. Will the conservation of energy be sustained as we approach the end of the universe? The notion of time and matter was always linked in my mind. What was before the big bang? Did time and matter always exist? If proton decay does not happen, will matter always exist?

The deliriums of an alcoholic father seem far removed from the events yet to unfold. Time will stop! The end will have arrived for us all. Let's catch the time machine and slow down. A method of my madness uncorked for all to see as we all traverse the magical rope we call life. We must get through this together. I am taking you along for the journey. You will not come out of this unscathed. You, too, will become embroiled with the mass of events yet to unfold.

The juggernaut of life to be explored by us all as we continue to parts unknown. The pearly gates will be there for us as the journey continues. We must reach deep into our souls and etch the memory of the present. All the presents make up the past. A cleansing of the id into a remorseful pitch is something to view. Take back the glory days and move with ever-quickening speed to the edge of the event horizon. Stare it down as if to say: "I told you so." You will not make a noodle out of me. Not this day. All the money will not make us happy. Work with wood and find contentment. Working with wood seems to relax many people; perhaps it has morphed over time to become a godsend. Perhaps it is true. Go west young man and find your glory.

Life is dealing with the mundane. One must try to keep active. That is one thing I learned on the farm. My father was always working and farming. He kept me busy as well. The long days in the field were punctuated by ice cold tea or lemonade once the chores were done. I can still see my father plowing the fields. The tractor belching and snorting as it continued plowing the field.

We are all fools believing in the talking heads of life, as if they know anything. They have all missed the boat. The Harvard mentality has gripped them well. The calculus of events unscrambled for us all to see. The apple has been peeled and the core is exposed. The worm seeks to escape, as it slithers from side to side. The Garden of Eden is ripe for the picking.

I wondered how Rico Inc was doing. I was missing Debbie

now. I missed our conversations. She seemed to set me straight on things. *This utter madness comes and goes. Sometimes, I think I am beginning to see the light. Deep in the cave, the light shows through. The persistence of the climb is numbed by the thought of the uncertainty principle. The discontinuous measurement of position and velocity will be determined by experimentation. When will we venture outside the cave to view the sun? The microscopic diodes and matching gowns trying to change the world is the catchword of the times.*

"Our time is up," Dr. Law said.

It has been a tiresome journey, but I am getting a sense of progress.

The unraveling of the mind is complicated. The days come and go with the ticking clock. The days are never recouped in the scheme of things. Soon the worms will take over and we will be as before, ashes of deposits of various sorts. The role of life repeated a billion times. To grasp the meaning of it is a life study. Seek and ye shall find becomes the rallying cry of today, tomorrow and forever. *Let it go, Charles,* I thought. Let it all go was something I knew I had to do. Say goodbye once and for all to this nonsense. No excuses, sir! Shaking moments of despair will cease and the sun will light your life. This is what I was hoping. Drink in the water from the stream, as it meanders through the ages. Don't be fooled by the weavers of bad tales but move with ever-quickening speed to the deliverance you seek.

CHAPTER 16

Since I had been writing, I had not seen Debbie that often. I told her I was writing, but I did not tell her what I was writing. I wanted to surprise her. I wanted her to read it and give me some of her ideas about the story. *I will broach the writing with her tonight at Saul's.* It was my plan to give her a copy to read.

When I started the story, it was my intent to have it published and perhaps make some money off it. I knew it was very difficult to get something published, especially for a first-time author. Debbie would be a good first-time reader of the story, I thought.

I had just finished my session with Dr. Law, and I was feeling a little nervous for some reason. I hadn't discussed anything of importance. I still had not talked to her about my snow dream. *Maybe next time,* I thought. I kept putting it off.

After my session, Debbie asked me to stop by and she would fix dinner. She was a good cook and I looked forward to seeing her. She made roast chicken with rice, a meal I always like. I was feeling a little drained after my session with Dr. Law. I told Debbie I was going to bed.

"Goodnight," she said.

"Goodnight."

I was tired from the walk, and it was nice to be in bed. Debbie had picked out a very comfortable bed. The pillows were made of goose down, and the bed was very comfortable. Soon, I fell into a deep sleep. It was not long before I entered the dream state.

The dream I had was bizarre:

I could see a black cloud coming toward me. In the background, as the cloud was coming nearer, a radio was playing. I was standing erect watching the black cloud approaching. Suddenly, the cloud became a swirling vortex. The cloud had formed into a tornado. It was moving at a high rate of speed. Jeff was yelling something to me. It was hard to hear him, as the noise from the tornado was crashing around me.

Then faintly, I heard my mother's voice say, "Lock the door." At this command, I walked over to the door and was going to lock it. The lock was green and very complicated. I grappled with it for a while but gave up. I couldn't lock it. My mother yelled again, "Lock the *door!*" I could now hear the radio. Someone on the radio was talking about war. Planes were flying overhead. Planes were crashing and tanks were moving forward. Ships were being sunk. There was general confusion everywhere. The door was still unlocked. I could not figure out how to lock the door.

I mentioned to Debbie about the dream I had during the night.

"By the way, I had a dream last night about locking a door. My mother was telling me to "Lock the door," a storm was coming."

"That's interesting. Maybe you should talk to Dr. Law about it," she said matter-of-factly.

"I am sorry. I shouldn't have bothered you with this."

"No problem, Charles. As I have told you before, I just

think things like this really need to be addressed with Dr. Law. We can talk about general ideas, but when things like dreams arise, it is best we not try to discuss them, as it could lead to erroneous conclusions on my part."

"I agree."

CHAPTER 17

*T*he next day, I received notification of my new investment. Goodbye Rico Inc.

The economics of investment is a tricky business. You always wonder if you are making the right decision. I didn't have a good feeling about the overall economy and the world economy in general. Because of the unstable currency markets and soft demand for many goods, I thought playing it safe for a while was a good choice.

When I told Debbie about my investing, she couldn't believe it. I told her the whole story about the options and my investment in Rico Inc and now my investment in SEATEC. She seemed shaken by what I told her.

"How could you do that, Charles? What happens if you lose it all, then what?"

"Yes, I know it is a real risk on my part, but I just need to try and make us more money."

"If we can't trust one another, what is the point of going on with this?"

I sat there for a while without speaking.

"I am sorry," I said.

"You should be."

I felt myself starting to shake. I was afraid I might be losing Debbie. Debbie sensed that I was having a difficult time in the moment.

"We just have to be on the same page."

"I agree, it won't happen again," I said.

The entire time being with Debbie, I never talked much to her about my background. I told her about my college years and a little about high school but nothing in detail about the abuse I suffered growing up at the hands of Jeff. At this point in our relationship, I didn't want to burden her with this background, although I sensed she could tell I might have had a hard time growing up. I also did not tell her about John Alexander, my biological father. I felt like I needed to tell her about this. I wondered how she would take it. It was like not telling her about the investment schemes. This was different, though, because in my mind this was a transformational event in my life. I was so afraid that this event would turn her against me. I always wondered if she discussed my situation with Dr. Law.

My job at First Financial Group was progressing. I was being given more responsibility and a few higher income accounts. I still thought that I was not going to make a lot of money working for commissions and a salary. That being the case, I began thinking of how to make more money in different ways. I started to think more outside the box.

My thinking was not just about making more money, but also about my relationship with Debbie. In the event she became my life partner, I wanted to give her a good life. I thought about us being together and all the things I wanted us to do as a couple. I knew I should talk to her more openly about our life together.

In addition to thinking about Debbie and our time together, my mind jumped to the import/export business, like my friend Joe had. Even though I told Debbie I wouldn't take any more risky business ventures, I felt the path I was now on was a safer path to making more money.

It wasn't long before the import/export business began to take off. I found myself doing business in India and San Francisco. The contacts were beginning to pay off. Paul had helped me stay focused and assisted me whenever he could.

My time with Debbie had again become less, due to how busy I was. It was Friday, and I was due to have my session with Dr. Law. I had been so busy, I almost forgot about the session altogether, which surprised me. I texted Debbie and asked if she would like to meet me at Saul's for dinner around 7:30 after my session. She said she would be there. She said she had not heard from me for a couple of weeks. She seemed upset and I could understand why she might be feeling angry with me. I told her in the text, I had been really busy and I would explain everything at Saul's.

"Dr. Law will see you now," Joan said.

Dr. Law was sitting in her usual place. She smiled briefly when I walked in. I sat down in my usual place, as well.

"How are you?" she asked.

"I feel OK."

She sat there looking at me. There was the usual silence. She was waiting for me to talk. I was thinking about what I wanted to discuss. Maybe the story I was writing or my business or about my locking the door dream and the storm. There were so many things running through my mind. I didn't want to talk about the story because I had not heard back from the editor, so I decided not to talk about that. The business was still in flux and it could fail miserably. I discussed the dream to see what she would say about it.

Her response was as follows:

She felt the relationship between the storm and the lock the door was significant. Her idea was that I was raging about Jeff. When my mother said to lock the door and I hesitated and couldn't lock the door, it was a sign that I am further separating myself from the situation I was in. The process of separation takes time. She said she had seen signs from me that the separation was ongoing. The fact that I was not talking about Jeff in therapy was one of the signs, as well as the fact that I was progressing with my life.

On reflection, it seemed to be a fairly straightforward analysis. The moving on with my life was certainly true and it was also true that I did not seem to talk about Jeff as much. She didn't say too much about John Alexander. Jeff Reed was the one who raised me.

I also began to consider that perhaps my time with Dr. Law might be coming to an end. It had been a long journey, but all things end, I reasoned. The idea of stopping therapy made me sad and happy, almost at the same time. I knew the time was drawing near. I did want Dr. Law, however, to be the one to end the weekly sessions. I felt she had the insight to know when it was over. The time would come.

I spoke to her about my business venture. I had mentioned to her that I was trying to start a new business, but I did not go into specifics. It was during this time I decided to leave First Financial Group. It was not easy telling Doug. He had been good to me and tried to move me along as fast as he could.

Although I really liked the Indian company I had become involved with, I needed to fill the orders faster. During the last three weeks, I sold the entire inventory of jeans and the Italian shoes were selling fast as well. Soon I was grossing more money than I thought possible. Much of this early success could be attributed to hard work and luck. I seemed to have the right products for the time. The struggle I went through in college was all worth it. I was on my way. The jeans and shoe business was booming but I had other ideas for another business.

"How are you?" Dr. Law asked.

"I am doing well."

As usual, she sat there waiting for me to say something.

"What do you think about my progress so far?" I asked.

"I think you have come a long way."

"What do you mean?"

"Charles, I have decided to relocate my practice to Southern California. This will be the last time we have together," she said.

"What should I do?"

"You will be fine," she said.

I was a little anxious at this moment.

"Should I find someone else?" I asked.

"What do you think?"

"I seem a lot better," I said.

"Well, maybe that is your answer."

"I think I will be OK."

I still had not talked to her about the snow dream. At this point, I would just let it go.

Perhaps the snow dream is one of those unresolved issues that will resolve on its own.

"I also think you will be OK," she said.

Her last words to me were, "The therapy continues".

When I got up to leave, she gave me a smile. I became choked up at the thought of not seeing Dr. Law again. The attachment to her was deep, as it should have been. All of the talking about my past, as well as trying to grapple with my unconscious mind, was complicated and was handled deftly by her. How could I ever thank her enough?

It didn't take long for me to start thinking about my life going forward. The fact I felt this way was good. The weaning away from the therapeutic process would take a while, but at least I had a starting point. The starting point I should have had in Dent.

I looked around the office for the last time. I noticed the painting with the squiggly lines going nowhere. Different colored lines. My mind was now focused and I just smiled and walked out. I didn't know if I would ever see Dr. Law again.

I immediately called Debbie and told her what happened. I told her what Dr. Law said and she agreed.

"I believe you have come a long way, as well. We can work things out together," she said.

CHAPTER 18

I missed Dr. Law and I tried to picture how she was doing in Los Angeles. It is funny how someone as important as Dr. Law can come into your life for such a time and then just vanish, never to be heard from again. I kept going over in my mind the comment she made to me about "The therapy continues."

After the many sessions, she gave me a good understanding of myself, and I would always remember her. I would have liked to see her again and show her the successes I was having. I knew she would smile. She helped me free the demons that were stopping me from achieving my goals. The interlude between therapy and self-analysis was difficult at first, but over time, you start to reconcile the fact that you are on your own. The idea of not seeing Dr. Law was like losing a good friend. I had my business and my story and, most of all, I had Debbie. I think Dr. Law would be proud.

Dr. Law instilled in me the difference between having a curiosity and interests. I always had curiosity, but I wasn't sure I had an interest in any one thing. I just seemed to be flitting around and trying to understand everything. It dawned on me that, if you look at the great successes, you will find that those who accomplish the most are the people who focus on one particular topic. The ability to focus was paramount to success. The first part, you have to have the curiosity — which hopefully you get from education, and then through curiosity, you find the interest, which will help you achieve your goals.

The ability to focus is important. There is a story about Einstein I remember reading. The story was about a prisoner who was taking calculus in prison. The prisoner came across a problem he could not solve. He sent a letter outlining the problem to Einstein. Einstein reviewed the problem and sent the problem back to the prisoner. The explanation did not solve the problem, but Einstein told the prisoner to keep working on it and focus. The prisoner did this and he was able to solve the problem. The prisoner sent a letter back to Einstein with the solution. He thanked Einstein in the letter.

The free flow of ideas came protruding out. *Will I ever have peace?* The incessant reformulations of events kept intruding into my essence. It will take a complete restructuring and reincarnation of us all. The process and events in crystallized form need to be addressed. We are all seeking resolutions. It's hard to be taken seriously. Who cares?

Are we getting smarter? Television might be killing our instinct to be curious. The cell phone of today taking our breath away will perhaps lead us to places we should not go. We are meandering into a sea of destruction because of our ignorance. Too many people lack the curiosity to go on. The unwavering soul will give in to the cocaine days and opium nights. The tranquility of the moment will circumvent the future, like the arching bending light of the universe. The curious minds will be no more as we sink into the harsh reality of what lies ahead. The enigma of the moment will be transcended into the night, searching for a place to stay. The crying years will be no more and laughter will only be a memory. The destruction of the worlds becomes all consuming, as it waits for the trigger to fire.

The synapse of life is gone and becomes muted into a mash of rope swinging from nowhere. We all seek to discover the answer to our cause.

What does it take to endure on this orb? A life filled with the ever-searching souls looking out at the cosmos. The swirling wind of change grasping at our essence is all encompassing. The happiness we find seems to be fleeting, as we try to capitalize on the glory of the moment. Time passes and transcends itself into the outer reaches of the mind.

The senses are enhanced by the opium of the moment. The numbness we seek to distort future realities. The good book has yet to be written of man's interlocking relationship with himself. Where will this take us? The rambling of ideas in a circular wheel were speeding along the arrow of time. Life is turning and moving slowly toward the unknown.

The bareness of life becomes exposed when we truly crack the genetic code. The genome will surprise us once we know the interconnecting cellular relationships. The immune system understood before our eyes. The basic trauma of getting on is still with us. Man's need to overcome and conquer will still prevail.

The meandering river of time succumbing to the erosion wrought on it by the one above. The thing we call the godhead peering down on us as if to judge us and our thoughts. One's thinking process of many billions of nerve cells slowly dying and evaporating into the cosmos.

The transition of life from the womb becomes imperiled by the creeping viruses that will plague us until the end. The laughter and gratification become muted as we further the unknown. What do we say to the stranger as we pass into the night?

CHAPTER 19

$\mathcal{T}$he idea of investing in a brewery in India was something Debbie and I discussed. She finally believed, to my great relief, that it might be a good idea. I reached a good agreement with Raj and his brother, Sabu, based on my seeing their brewery in India first hand.

The flight from San Francisco to Kolkata landed smoothly. The airport was small compared to most. In fact, our plane was only one of two in the entire airport. Sabu, Raj's brother, came to Kolkata to meet me. The plan was to spend a few days in Kolkata to recover from the twenty-two hour flight. We would then take the train together to Jamshedpur to the brewery.

India is a country of one billion people. While in Kolkata, I noticed beggars seeking rupees from the walking masses. Some of the beggars were children and some were as young as six or seven years of age. Sabu said that most of the beggars were of the lower caste. I had heard about the caste system before when I took a course in world history in college. I was seeing the effects of it first hand in Kolkata.

The wretchedness of it and the smell was overpowering.

The caste system kept many Indian people under the thumb of the higher order. It was a poor way to model a society. The degradation and despair felt by many Indians was offset by the few who could experience the good life. I wondered if most of the Indian people were fooled into believing they didn't deserve the good life. It was a devious disorder couched in the name of religion. The masses had been engulfed in a cloud of imaginary smoke, breathed in by the aristocrats, who became addicted to the notion of superiority and enhancement for their own cause.

The landscape of India was filled with sacred cows moving at their own leisure through the rural areas and cities. Sacred cows were not to be messed with, unless you wanted to cause a riot. The sight of cows within Kolkata surprised me. Even in the city, cow dung was scooped up by those who used it for cooking. The cow dung was their coal, the fuel of their life. India was filled with stories of riots between Muslims and Hindus over the issue of sacred cows. Life in India is hard for many of the people. Is religion one of the factors needed for a sense of survival? Religion was indeed the drug of the people, as Marx indicated in his writings.

We arrived at our inn in Jamshedpur where we would stay for the next four days. It was a very small inn, called the Beldih Club, and only had about ten rooms, which were very nice and large. I had a large TV and a queen size bed. There was a small desk as well as a cooler with a supply of drinks and assorted nuts to eat. Across the street from the Beldih Club was a high school. The school was a Jesuit school that used to be run by American Jesuits but was now run by Indian Catholics. According to Sabu, it was a very good school. Actually, he said that the school offered two years of college as well high school. It started in kindergarten. *Interesting*, I thought.

Jamshedpur was a city of about one million people. Jamshedpur was built by Tata Corporation, the huge Indian conglomerate. There was a huge steel mill located just outside of the city. It was my understanding that American engineers were the ones who built the mill in the mid fifties. Sabu informed me that Jamshedpur planted over one million trees about fifteen years ago. Jamshedpur was now a lush and thriving city.

The club offered a swimming pool and a bar that was just to the left side of the building proper. Just in the back of the club was a lush golf course with green rolling hills. It was beautiful.

Sabu and I decided to meet up in the bar area. Once inside the bar, there were ten stools and about six or seven tables located just behind the bar. The bar was carpeted with a deep red Berber material. At one end of the bar was a colorful scripture from Seva. There was also a picture of Nehru, the first leader of India after the overthrow of the English in 1947. Sabu and I took a table and ordered some tea and nuts.

"What do you think of Jamshedpur?" he asked.

"What I have seen so far, I am impressed," I said.

"Tomorrow we will go and see how the brewery is doing," he said.

We talked for a while in the bar and then called it an evening. We were both tired from the long train ride from Kolkata.

My stay in Jamshedpur was delightful. I enjoyed meeting Sabu and thought that if I ultimately decided to make the investment, it would be well-managed.

The trip back to Kolkata was accomplished by train. I told Sabu that I would take the train back myself and spend the rest of my time looking around Kolkata. He drove me to the train station and we said our goodbyes.

"It was really great meeting you, Sabu. Thank you for showing me around Jamshedpur and I enjoyed our talk yesterday," I said.

"Same here, all round," Sabu said.

We shook hands and I boarded the train. It would take six hours to reach Kolkata. As the train pulled away, Sabu gave me a wave and smile. So nice, I thought.

The train ride back to Kolkata was a good time for me to continue to reflect on things. I had a first class seat and therefore, I had quite a bit of privacy. I could look out of the train window and see the people going about their business for the day. There was a highway that ran alongside the train track and the cars were beginning to bunch up as they were making their way to somewhere. On the other side of the tracks was a path where bicycles and scooters zipped along. We were still some distance away from Kolkata, so I assumed there must have been smaller towns along the way.

There is one thing about being out of the country; you often reflect on some of the problems which you think need addressing. At least for me, I contemplated these problems and tried to reconcile in my mind some probable solutions. I suppose you could say it was a game I played with myself. It was in my nature to dissect things and be curious about ideas. It wasn't long before a barrage of thinking and spewing of thoughts emerged. I could not ever seem to control it. Perhaps it was part of my internal makeup.

This is what I was feeling while on the train chugging along to Kolkata. I wished I could somehow wave a magic wand over America and make it ideal. Yes, I say ideal. Why not seek the ideal? The thinking process can create emotional stressors. Sometimes the body shakes from the obvious revelations which might be forthcoming.

The problems of America are bare and open to discussion. The distribution of wealth has gone astray and capitalism prevails. The control of labor becomes the mantra of corporations, as unions start to lose their grip in the representation of their members. The top one percent own forty percent of the wealth in America.

Racism runs rampant and becomes a yoke for the black and brown, preventing many of them from achieving the American dream. The Harvard types send their kids to college in a never-ending stream, seeking their way to the land they were promised from the start. The capital way of believing in the good life, as America's working class is beaten down to apathy. The sinking mind of America needs to be lifted up and brushed off. Many Americans wonder where they will get their next meal. We need a rejuvenation of mind and spirit in America.

The train chugged along, stopping every so often to unload and board passengers. Onward I go, trying to fathom the spiral of thinking on which I seem to be focused. We need a wake-up call. A call to order is due. Inherited wealth runs rampant. America is a caste system, like India, just under a different mask. Make everyone whole. That is the ideal, but is it achievable? The outsiders try to get into the elite of society but the trek will be circumscribed by the mighty rich. The unsmiling ones who hold sway over the masses.

The train was only a few miles from Kolkata. I spent the night at the Grand Hotel. I kept going over my meeting with Sabu and I again thought everything went well. I enjoyed our conversation at the Beldih Club. I always like talking about science and biology. I missed Debbie and was so looking forward to seeing her. My feeling was that I was excited about investing in the brewery in Jamshedpur. It was pretty much my decision to make.

When I got to my room, I decided to take a hot shower and watch TV and relax. The bed was comfortable and the flat screen TV was right in front of the bed. *Nice.*

The dream I had in Jamshedpur seemed complicated when it

came to mind, so I put it aside and was hoping perhaps Debbie could try to figure it out. On the other hand, I thought maybe I would try to analyze it, myself. I should not use the word "analyze" because that to me indicates a good knowledge of the dream process and what is involved. The fact I had read many psychological books, especially Freud's book on dream theory, didn't make me some kind of analyst. The dream I had in India about a plane flying into the weeds was interesting to me. The fact there were mansions involved also pricked my curiosity.

Following is what I came to suspect about the dream:

The plane flying through the weeds represented me getting into the business. I was getting into the nitty-gritty of the business operations on many fronts. The fact that the plane was flying so low was that the business was still in a nascent stage. When I got out and was directing it, it was me directing the business. The idea of going up and seeing mansions and the ocean was somewhat of a projection of what could happen if I became highly successful.

The reason I relate it all to the business is because this is what was on my mind. I still wanted to ask Debbie about the dream. I wasn't sure why I was so interested in dreams. Maybe it was because they represented unlocked secrets, which were dormant and unavailable to the conscious mind. Dreams represented a mystery to me. Dreams were like the uncorked lava of a spewing volcano spilling over after a million years. Spewing lava, seeking revenge for being pent up for so long, seemed like an apt description.

The Grand Hotel was a stately old hotel. Each room had a balcony where you could see the city below. I only had a few days before I would be leaving India. What would be the memories that would stay with me? Perhaps it was the first evening when Sabu came to my room and we both sat on my balcony and talked.

I could string together the ideas of that time in my mind.

The clouds were red, and twilight was almost upon us. The stars were becoming visible as Sabu and I sat there together, each with our own reflections of what was happening before us. The serenity had a calming effect on me, and we were both feeling comfortable after our conversations about everything. I recalled the heat of the day was subsiding, and a gentle breeze pulled at our bodies, giving us a respite from the day's heat.

I tried to conjure up what Debbie was doing. In a flash of the moment, I also considered the beggars of India and where they would be tonight. I stared down at the city below. The money lenders of India unexpectedly cropped up. They represented the Mafia of India. Not all of them, but enough to make you wonder about humanity. Usury on a grand scale, and it had the effect of usurping the unsuspecting soul. The cessation of the heat was good for now but would only last a short while until it would again become a seamless eternalness of tomorrow.

The trip from the Grand Hotel to the airport gave me another perspective. I was somewhat taken aback by sights I could never have imagined living in San Francisco. I was being sheltered from the storm of humanity that was groping for existence in the infinity of the space and time continuum, of which we are all a part.

I was energized by this new environment. I saw Indian women walking along the road, carrying up to thirteen bricks on their heads. The sound of music coming from somewhere unknown to me added an Asian flavor. Sing-song Indian music blared into the night, and I just wondered what it meant. What was the story it was trying to tell, I mused. Indian music seemed to grab me. It shook me up for some unknown reason.

A spell had been cast, and I became enchanted with this Asian land. The men squat to relieve themselves of the rice and curry and milkshake tea and maybe a little vodka along the way. The jungle people beat their drums in the night. They scurry back and forth to build a night fire for cooking and for whatever suits them. The jungle people would go into their huts for lovemaking, where the children come too soon. The little begging heads with no chance for Cambridge. Only the cobra-infested jungle is where these people will call home.

The denominator of untouchables of Indian society were being left out, and the controlling elite who were going on their merry way. The Indian bureaucracy ruled the day. As Sabu told me, the bureaucracy was strangling the life out of the average Indian. These were the memories I was having. Indelible memories of India that would last a lifetime was something I would cherish.

I did talk to Sabu for quite some time on the balcony of the Grand Hotel in Kolkata. I would never forget Jamshedpur either. It was a beautiful city that Tata created. The planting of so many trees was something that should be done in America. The nice inn at the Beldih Club was delightful.

There is such oneness of humanity. We are one on this planet. The grip of political systems on societies oftentimes keeps us separated. What is the solution to this conundrum? It seems to me that religion plays a central part in keeping humanity separated. I thought about what I found out in India when the Hindus and Muslims go to war with each other. By studying religion, you begin to realize how religion has affected mankind in a deleterious way over the ages. One just has to look at the battles that went on for so many years between the Catholics and Protestants. The story goes on and the upheaval caused by religion is ongoing.

I also thought about the manipulation of the mind. How do people succumb to the cult of personality? Many people have a need to be controlled from the top. We are now confronted with the notion of human nature. The ontology of the mind foisted upon us out of necessity. It will become evident, as the world's population continues to expand, that a fundamental shift in thinking will have to be forthcoming. A global management structure must be put into place. If we are not able to control the deleterious forces that man is inflicting on the environment, we will not survive. We can't survive.

CHAPTER 20

*A*fter my recent trip, I had some free time to reflect on the journey. I turned on the radio next to my bed and opted for some smooth jazz. It was nice being back in my bed in the city I loved.

I was enthralled at the robustness of this faraway land. There were, however, signs that all was not as glowing as I had imagined. The overpopulation was very evident there, especially in Kolkata. The result of the overpopulation and smog was becoming unbearable. The other facet that was concerning was hygiene. The train ride from Jamshedpur to Kolkata offered an opportunity to observe this lack of hygiene. I could see people relieving themselves right in the open. It was not a pleasant sight. Hygiene becomes extremely important as the population of the planet grows. This is especially true for overpopulated areas such as India and China.

Raj texted: "Welcome back, Charles. How about we meet on Tuesday? Raj"

I texted back: "OK, how about 9 AM? Charles."

Raj texted back: "Roger. See you then."

All that being done, I decided to take a quick nap before

starting the day. Soon I was caught up in an extraordinary dream.

The dream unfolded as follows:

I was lost in the jungle. There were trees and shrubs everywhere. Cobras were slithering past me. The roar of the tigers could be heard in the background. The sounds of birds became amplified as they seemed to warn me of the events that were about to unfold. My ears rang from the noise they were making. The full force of the jungle was crying out in the night, and I could hear the beat of drums in the distance. Fires burned everywhere. The entire jungle was on fire. I ran with all speed to seek shelter from the fires. The people of the jungle yelled and screamed at a high pitch. They looked for shelter from the fire.

I swam in a lake. I tried to get to the other side. All at once, I was pulled under the water and found myself in an underwater cavern. There were old markings on the walls of the cavern. It appeared there were life-forms that lived there eons ago. I lay down on the cave floor to rest, but soon I was inundated with cobras.

They were trying to penetrate me! They were going into my body, deeper and deeper, and there was no way I could stop them. I tried to call out, but no one was listening. There was silence. Complete silence. The cobras were still in me.

I reached into my mouth and pulled a cobra out. I bit off its head and threw it into the fire in front. The cobras hissed at the jungle people as they were making their way into the cavern, trying to avoid the big fire above.

I wanted to help them, but I was now a cobra and could only hiss at them as they entered the cave. I slithered away into the depths of the cavern. I went into small spaces where only a cobra could go. I soon encountered a female cobra, and it had a face like Debbie's. I swayed in front of her. The dream continued as we were swaying to a love dance being played by drums above.

The beginning of time was before us, and India was but a speck of dust before the big bang. Undulating turmoil was awash with free quarks searching for the start. Cosmos time standing still until the event of creation happened. The racing mind stopped until the new day came. The zygotes of tomorrow were but a thought of the moment seeking its own life-form. Perfect symmetry achieved where physics was nowhere to be found.

I awoke sweating profusely, as usual. It seemed like I sweated a lot after my dreaming episodes. Dr. Law would have had something to say about this dream. What did the dream mean? It was the kind of dream I didn't think I would have again. Was this a setback for me? I thought I was doing so well. Maybe I should contact Dr. Law in Los Angeles and try to set up an appointment. Then I remembered what she said: "The therapy continues." I would have to try and figure this dream out on my own. I knew it obviously had something to do with India, but the interrelationship between India and science was hard for me to understand. Science seemed to be so endemic in my personality. Trying to get a handle on nature was so complex.

I immersed myself in the concepts of the cobras and fire and the jungle in India. Since I had just come from India, this part did not surprise me. The notion of the people in the jungle also did not surprise me. The fact that I turned into a cobra was what I was unable to discern. Why a cobra? Why not a Bengal tiger? In my mind, the king cobra is what identifies India to me for some reason. It is a symbolism that is ancient to India.

During my conversation with Sabu, when I was in Jamshedpur, he did mention that a cobra was found slithering through the golf course which was just behind where we were staying. He said some kids tried to catch it but it went into a hole and escaped. I didn't pay it much mind at the time, but perhaps this is how the cobras came into my dream state. Sometimes a little pinch like that can have an influence on you. Was it really a setback, or was it a growth dream?

The fact that Debbie was also a cobra was another aspect of the dream I didn't understand. Perhaps I had become completely imbued with India. The poverty and the inequities I saw there apparently resonated with me. The fact that Debbie was with me in the dream and was also a cobra could denote the closeness I was feeling toward her. Debbie had become a part of me. We were cobras together. This is the way I wanted it. Making love as cobras, with India as the backdrop, seemed comfortable to me. It showed my love for Debbie was growing stronger and that there was nothing that could stand in the way.

I wanted Debbie to go with me to India. I wanted her to experience this land that I fell in love with, and I was sure she would love it too. It was hard to imagine that I could feel this way about a country after such a short time. I was missing it now and I was looking forward to meeting with Raj. My attitude had now changed about him. I could see how the Sikhs were the leaders in India. They were the merchants, in some cases the money men making money with money. I left India with a lot of respect for them.

CHAPTER 21

*P*erhaps the dream was trying to warn me about something. The thrust of the dream centered on India. Nevertheless, it seemed to have an impact on me. I just could not put it all together. Since I was no longer in therapy, maybe I could run it by Debbie. I felt reluctance about doing this, though.

Because the business was starting to take off, I considered relocating from my current apartment and shopping around for a condo in the city. I needed to call Debbie and let her know.

The cobra dream was fading. *Maybe I should just let it go into the ether. Regroup and keep on moving on,* I thought. The snow dream, however, was different. In a way this dream still haunted me. I had to keep thinking about it. I had to somehow resolve it.

One of the ideas that I discussed with Dr. Law had to do with the fear of success. Her analysis was one of the ideas we discussed. The emotional complexity of this was hard for me to understand.

"Charles, because of the abuse at the hands of Jeff, this

emotional experience has created a fear of success in you. The confidence you had in yourself was shaken at a young age. This is not uncommon for someone with your background. But we can try to resolve this through talking about it. You should be aware of this going forward."

I did think about it over the years since she told me this. I wondered again about the dream. Maybe this Indian cobra dream was the fear of success that Dr. Law talked to me about years ago. I began to see what Dr. Law meant when she said "The therapy continues."

It was always nice to walk to Debbie's apartment. It was a lovely evening and the stars were out in all their glory. We walked hand in hand. We walked past Dr. Law's old office and where Debbie now had her practice. She was able to get a good office at a good price. There were other professionals in the building as well. Seeing the building brought back memories. I was feeling satisfied with myself at how everything was going. I felt as though I was becoming successful. I began to realize that the dream was trying to put a fear in me: the fear of success. *I will conquer this on my own. Now Debbie and I will make love and I will move on with my life with Debbie. There is so much to do.*

CHAPTER 22

*D*ebbie's practice was doing well. Her practice was making over $10,000 per month. Because her patient portfolio was increasing at a fast pace, she had to relocate to another office. She was able to get out of her lease at the Fillmore office. It was nice to see Debbie becoming successful. She put in a lot of hard work, and it was starting to pay off for her.

I did not talk to Debbie that much about my background, especially the abuse part. She knew some of the basic things, and she helped me interpret one of my dreams.

One of the ideas I learned when I studied psychology was that it was hard for a significant other to engage in psychological analysis. Since we were both imbued with psychological interest, we knew that analysis between us was not something we should engage in. Couples tend to be too emotionally attached, and it was too difficult to make a proper evaluation of each other. She realized this and therefore did not engage in any kind of therapeutic analysis. She did help me, though, by just being the kind of person she was. We both had respect for each other. We were able to laugh at each other and at the world as well. Because our lives were so busy now, we did cherish our time together.

Just as I was feeling so great about everything, something came over me like a dark cloud. All of a sudden, I was struck by a memory from the past. It was snowing heavily, and the outside temperature was twenty below zero. It had been snowing solidly for about two days. We had the fire on and Lou and I were doing homework. It was about 6 PM and it was dark outside. From outside, we heard a car door slam. My father had come home.

"You and Lou should go to your room, Charles, and lock your door," my mother said.

We went into my room. It wasn't long before we heard my mother and father arguing with each other. This was strange for me because usually my mother would not argue with Jeff. In fact, this was one of the few times that I heard her argue back with him. It was not a pleasant thing to hear, and I was embarrassed for Lou that he had to hear this. I felt so sorry for my mother. I knew Jeff had been drinking. Soon there was a pounding on my door.

"Charles, get your ass out here," Jeff yelled.

"What do you want?" I yelled back.

I locked the door as my mother told me to do when I heard the yelling begin.

"I want you to shovel the snow off the driveway," he said.

"It's too cold out," I yelled back.

"You are such a sissy," he said.

There was silence. He walked away. I was shaking from the confrontation. Lou came over and hugged me and then left. Now I was alone with my thoughts on this snowy night.

It was a clear night in San Francisco, and I started to reflect on Jeff in Dent. It wasn't pleasant. My mind recoiled into a rage and then spewed uncorked for all to see. The tigers are hungry, as they search for food deep in the jungles of India. My thinking started to ramp up and take new turns.

The problems are mounting and the planet will come crashing down in the coming years. If it happened to the dinosaurs, it can happen to us. Fires are brewing amid the hinterland. The growing masses will seek refuge to a better place. Eden is a faraway dream and has now become unachievable.

The path forward will take a massive change in the conduct of humanity. Some stark changes will have to be made. The religious model might have to be reevaluated or even abandoned, to enable the measures that will have to be taken to resolve the impending doom. The population of the planet will have to be reduced by billions of people. Yes, I said billions. Each couple will be limited to one child. The pollution of the planet will have to be addressed. Severe penalties will have to be assessed for corporations and people who pollute. Diseases will become more rampant and more potent. The global economies will be hard-pressed to cope with the pandemics that will surely come. The scientists can only do so much. It will depend on all of us to combat the gloomy world that is coming very fast. Education will become extremely important.

The dual relationship between capitalism and democracies are ideas that have to be reconciled. Capitalism can be good but there can also be discontinuities that have to be addressed. Some sort of equality has to be made between those who conquer the notion of the capitalistic system to those who can't compete. Extreme capitalism can cause revolutions. The people will rise up and try to overthrow those in power. The disparity in America will be felt at the elections of people who offer panaceas which are unattainable.

This lack of education becomes prevalent during the election process. This becomes the feeding ground for charlatans who will try to placate the uneducated and, with the wrong person elected to office, a totalitarian event could occur. A streaming line into the unknown is before us. I am trying to figure out what can lead us to action in making life on the planet enjoyable. Why should we accept less? We must get off this slippery slope into oblivion. Who will take charge and lead? Are there answers? Do we need an entirely new mode of governance?

Karl Marx was searching for a solution in his time. Perhaps he came close but, no cigar, my friend. He saw the disparity in the nineteenth century and he tried to resolve it. The rich and poor disparity kept widening and Marx was trying to resolve the problem. His thinking generated a revolution in Russia and ushered in communism. We must review the history. Are there intellectuals that can come up with a better system? If not, we are doomed. Doomed like the dinosaur who roamed this planet for 175 million years. Putting oil in our cars is not the answer and is becoming our downfall.

Being successful seems to be hard for me. Trying to overcome the past is difficult at best. My upbringing had a limiting effect on what I thought I could achieve. My beaten-down life did not warrant success. I noticed that when I was successful at something, it upset me. When I got an A on a midterm exam in high school, it made me upset. This idea of success was reflected in the dream I had the other night. It was a creepy dream.

The dream unfolded as follows:

I found myself adrift in a sea of worms. Squiggly worms were trying to get inside me like the cobras of past dreams. I beat them off. They were slimy with big eyes filled with a desire to eat me. I was killing them as fast as I could. There was a never-ending stream of them. I rose up and jumped on them.

Then the spiders came. Black widows and tarantulas with big hairy legs came down on me and I was caught in a spider web and could not get out. I felt that death was only moments away. A huge spider crawled down into the web where I was stuck. The spider had green eyes and a big poison sac. It looked like the deadly Australian spider. It seemed like it was going to devour me totally. I kicked and screamed, trying to get out of the web.

When I awoke, I felt weak, as in other dreams.

The knock on the door, and the fear of Jeff I felt so many years ago, was probably the root cause of this dream. It must be the unconscious self coming to life seeking revenge on my soul. I thought the dream was telling me I can't be successful. The dream was trying to smack me down: You don't have what it takes. You are a big "sissy" still rang in my memory on that cold, snowy night in Dent.

Don Silvatori, my Italian contact, gave me a list of shoes he thought would sell in the U.S. I told Phil, my operations manager, to check out what items he thought would sell and see if he agreed with Don. I did trust Phil's judgment and thought he would come up with the answer.

Because of the brewery in Jamshedpur I texted Sabu: "How are things progressing with the brewery?"

It was not long before he returned my query. "Hi, Charles, we are about a month off. Will you be coming to the opening?"

"Debbie and I are planning to come."

"Great, see you soon," he said.

I keep getting back to the big idea theme. Who would suffer should the big idea go into effect? Big oil and the automobile industry would certainly suffer. These industries have to restructure their businesses. In the U.S., mass transit would have to be ramped up. Automobiles would have to be completely free of emitting CO_2 into the atmosphere. We must transition out of coal and other toxic materials. The planet must heal. The world addiction to the automobile must be broken. These are known facts, but who is listening? This big idea just came over me after I texted Sabu. My conversations with Sabu were invigorating to say the least.

Debbie and I met at the bar in the building where we now lived. Debbie had just finished with her last patient and I had more things in the fire, business-wise. We were both feeling good about everything. Debbie's practice was doing well, as she now had more than thirty patients. Her office situation was working out. We loved our condo and the view we had was just wonderful. Kate, my office manager, was doing well. She was signing up clients each day at a good clip. I told her I was going to expand the agency business and that we would probably have to get more office space. I told her we could get more office space in the same building. She liked the idea.

CHAPTER 23

The dream was as follows:

The road was straight. It was a two-lane road. I was the only car on the road. On each side of the road were tumbleweeds. In the distance, I could see a town. The town was located on my right side. As I approached the town, I could see a road that turned into the town. I made the right turn and headed toward the town. The tumbleweeds soon vanished. The sun was in its last phase and starting to set. As I approached the town, there was a barn-like building. There was writing on the building that I could not make out. The building was located to my left side as I made a right turn and headed into the center part of the town. The town had a variety of stores located on each side. It was an old town. The town had wooden walkways on each side. It was a scene you might see in an old western movie. A few people walked along on the wooden walkway. They seemed happy, as they were laughing and talking together.

There was a restaurant on my left side. I stopped the car and got out. I was very thirsty. I walked into the restaurant and sat down at a large table. The server came over to my table. When I looked at the person, I saw my mother. She was waiting on me. I could not speak. I went mute. She did not recognize me. I felt hurt and started crying. I got up from the table. I was still thirsty.

I walked toward where I parked the car. The car was not there. I strode up and down the street looking for the car. I then reached for my cell phone with the idea of calling the police. Had the car been stolen? When I tried to call the police, all the numbers started to run together into one large mass. I could not call.

I woke up. I had fallen asleep on the couch. Debbie had not come home yet. I went out on the balcony and took in the view of the city. Like in my dream, the sun was setting, and you could see the reflected glow off the skyscrapers which were located all around our building.

I was going to talk to Debbie about the upcoming trip to Jamshedpur in a month or so. I was pleasurably anticipating going back to India. There was something magical about it. The vibrancy and smells were something to behold. This was especially true in Kolkata. The rickshaws and scooters going every which way was the scene locked into my brain. The sing-song music was crying out for answers. It was a different life plan and was in stark contrast to what is found in most of the world, particularly in America.

During the next week, Raj and I met with Dean Jasper, the lead guy for Virgo Space One Corporation. We sealed the deal. I asked Raj if it was OK if I had my attorney draw up the agreement between us. He said he had no objection. When the agreement was ready, we met at Jake's on Union Street and signed it.

"Are you celebrating something?" Jim, the bartender, asked.

"We are celebrating our new venture," I said.

We toasted each other and shook hands. We had a good discussion.

"By the way, I have never met your wife," I said.

When I said that, he pulled out his billfold and showed me her picture. She was a pretty woman with long black hair. The picture showed her in a flowery sari of different colors.

"She is beautiful. Will she be going to India for the opening of the brewery?" I asked.

"Yes, she will be going."

"Will Debbie be going?"

"Yes."

"How long will you be staying?" I asked.

"We are going to stay two weeks. How many days will you stay?"

"I was thinking five to seven days, but we may stay longer. Where are you staying in Jamshedpur?" I asked.

"We will be staying at the Beldih Club, where you stayed when you were there," Raj said.

"I guess we should be making reservations, as it doesn't have many rooms," I said.

"No worries, Sabu will take care of it. Just let him know the dates and he will make the necessary plans," he said.

"I really appreciate Sabu's efforts. I will make the reservation for our stay in Kolkata," I said.

"Will you stay at the Grand again?" Raj asked.

"No, I think we will stay at the Oberoi Hotel this time."

"Nice hotel," he said.

"Why don't you and Beth come over to our place for a little get-together?" I asked.

"We would love that," he replied.

"OK, I will talk to Debbie and we will set it up."

"Great!"

"By the way, my mother's name was Beth," I said.

"Really interesting," he said.

After we got a final date for the opening, we made the reservation for the airplane and the Oberoi in Kolkata. We decided we could stay six days. This was the amount of time Debbie could be away. Everything was in place, I thought.

It would not be long before Debbie and I would be soaring in the clouds headed for India. Notions of the mind became a force which permeated my soul. I seem to need to regurgitate these ideas to free my mind.

The onslaught starts:

Give myself to nature. Become a hermit in the woods and succumb to the handouts from those who believe in the cosmic order of it all; a lonely soul walking through the woods looking for an albatross that is making its way to the sea. The growing mind filled with a need to be alive. Looking for answers from a different perspective seems like the only alternative to balance out reality for a new day.

Asking different questions is important to fully grasp this new paradigm. Separating the facts from the fiction of life becomes the mantra. Forget the atomistic theories and view the pine needles under the feet of life. The running sap from the huge pine trees ripping along the waterfront creates a breath of fresh air we all want. The swirling water of life becomes a chiming metaphor wanting to be touched by a troubled soul. The incessant chant of "come to me, touch me, caress me, hold me tight and forever" is forever etched in my memory. The true aura of life unfolding, the grasshoppers are jumping and the wasps circling their nests, waiting for the right time to snuggle. Bees are buzzing and nectar flowing from the flowering petals of red and green and blue.

A big buck stood there, staring at me, and I stared back. The big eyes from another life-form were smiling at me as if to say: "Where have you been?" The newborn fawn taking its first steps; which was a shaky start to a new dawn. The gifts of the gods were before me. Is this what I have been looking for? The unending scheme of life played out for all to see.

A new philosophy could be unfolding for us to examine in detail. Forget the money. The selfish regurgitations will come to an end if we are not careful. Care about others and it will give you a new life. The curious mind wandering around Walden Pond looking for its master is the theme for the day. The small creatures may not have a chance for survival in this madness of the planet, searching for their own identity. You can watch the firefly glowing in the dark, as if it were showing us a different view of things. The fluttering singing wrens, feeding their young high in the trees, watching humanity form our reality below. You can see the snakes slithering along, not caring about anything except finding their hole to hide. The dreams of despair lost in the ripple of the water cascading over the rocks into the magical pond.

All the tragedies of tomorrow; succumbing to the ripples of the water falling over the rocks of time. No more night-mare nights filled with the scum of uncertainty. We might be faced with the fluffy clouds smiling at us, egging us on. Perhaps there is a future after all, I thought.

There was a buzz over the intercom in our unit.

"Yes," I replied.

"You have a couple by the name of Raj Singh wanting to see you. Is it OK?" said the front desk.

"Yes, they are fine, thank you," I said.

The protocol for entry into most buildings was pretty strict ever since the 9/11 event. Although it happened years ago, there was still the residue of distrust and wariness among the world's population. Often, people talk about the tragedy as if it happened yesterday. We did have a good visit with Raj and Beth.

After Raj and Beth left, I decided to give a call to the detec-tive agency. I had been thinking about making the call for some time. I just wanted to wait until the right time to tell Debbie.

"Josh Phillips Detective Agency," was the reply on the phone.

"My name is Charles Reed. I was wondering if you can find a person I have been trying to find for a number of years. I haven't had much luck."

"Yes, this is something we can do," she said.

"What do you need from me to get started?"

After giving the agency the data they requested, I figured on how long it would take to find John Alexander.

CHAPTER 24

*I*t was Saturday, and Debbie and I had just finished our breakfast when I asked her to take a ride.

"Sure. Where to?" she asked.

"Just a ride," I said.

About 6 PM we decided to take the ride. I headed down Highway 280 toward San Jose.

"Are we going to San Jose?" Debbie asked.

"Not all the way."

After I drove to the Woodside turnoff, I doubled back, going toward San Francisco.

"Where in the world are we going?" Debbie asked again.

"You will see."

As we approached the turnoff, the sun was setting. I could sense that Debbie now knew where we were going. When I turned to go up the off-ramp, she knew for sure.

"Oh Charles, what's in your head?" she asked.

"You will see," I said as I continued up the off-ramp.

When I pulled into the final spot, I asked Debbie if we could get out of the car.

"You really like it here, don't you?" Debbie said.

"Do you remember we made love here?"

"Of course I remember," she said.

We stood together watching the glow of the sunset in the west. It was a fairly warm night, and I decided the time was right to ask. I got down on my knee.

"Debbie, will you marry me?"

"Oh, Charles, of course I will. What a beautiful ring, Charles."

"I am glad you like it."

I stood up and gave her a kiss. We sat down on the leaves under the trees and watched the final end of the day. The aura of the moment captured the tenderness: a once in a lifetime commitment promised by a kiss.

"There is something I want to tell you," I said.

"What is that?"

"I found out in my last year of high school that Jeff Reed is not my biological father."

"How did you find this out?"

"My mother told me," I said.

"Have you tried to find your biological father?"

"I have tried to find him but I have not had any luck. I just hired a detective agency."

"Thanks for finally telling me," she said, as she looked away.

"I know I should have told you sooner, but I didn't know how you would take it."

"How did you think I would take it?"

"I just wasn't sure."

"Well, you should have told me sooner."

After she calmed down after telling her about John, we were able to recapture the moment of the proposal. I probably should have told her at a different time, but I wanted her to know everything before she truly accepted my proposal.

It was then I knew I was the right one for her.

"I am so happy, Charles," she said.

"I am too."

"I just love my ring."

"I think we should try to marry as soon as we get back from India. Do you think we should have a large wedding?" I asked.

"Not really."

"You know what just dawned on me? Perhaps we could get married in Jamshedpur, India," I said.

"Really?" she said.

"Sure, why not?"

"That would be wonderful," she said.

"I will set it up."

I purchased the flight tickets for India and made reservations for our two-day stay at the Oberoi in Kolkata. We decided to stay six days total in India, as this was the maximum time Debbie could be away from her practice. I again got business class seating for the twenty-two hour flight. Debbie and I were getting excited about going. We'd stay in Kolkata for two nights and fly into Jamshedpur. We thought we would take the train back to Kolkata after the stay in Jamshedpur.

Before we left, I told Sabu that Debbie and I wanted to get married in Jamshedpur. He said he could arrange for one of the priests at Loyola to marry us. I asked Debbie if that would work for her. She said that would be fine. Sabu made the arrangements for us. We were both excited for this to happen. It would be so memorable.

CHAPTER 25

I contemplated selling the company and retiring. It was fleeting, but nonetheless, it was coming in flashes. How much could I get for the business? I dreamed about the rest of my life with Debbie. I was wondering if Debbie would be willing to travel at some point. I was older than Debbie, so she probably wanted to work longer. Perhaps we could just start taking more trips. I supposed I could do some writing.

My mind again digressed:

There are so many things that need changing. Maybe someday we will all come together as one, as they say. The explosion of the mind should be heeded. We are all crying out for solutions, but the cries land on deaf ears. At what point do the people rise up and say, "No more! We want solutions now!" The raging must be had by all on a global scale. The planet is suffering and needs our help or it will succumb to the taunts of the grim reaper waiting in the wings. A common language is needed so we dispel the myths that will be coming our way.

Science must be listened to and be followed. We owe

science much, as we cower under the threat of nuclear war. The invention of the automobile, as I keep saying, becomes the suffocating factor that is moving us to the point of oblivion. We need to catch our breath. The diesel generators in New Delhi spewing out smoke that rises into the pretentious sky that is seeking relief from all the other particles that are unknown to us. The belching from the coal mines is seeking to further destroy us all.

Political systems unwilling to confront the problems we all face. A convergence of all political systems must come together and rectify the threat that is now and is growing exponentially. Many themes keep repeating over and over. Desperate souls seeking revenge from the moment, we must keep the repetition going as it relates to our survival.

Jamshedpur, in many ways, does not truly represent India but Kolkata does. We would be in Kolkata for two days and I thought it was enough time for Debbie to get some idea of what I had been telling her.

I know I used to drive her crazy about my fear of viruses. It has been my view that the viruses would start in China or India. The overarching reasoning was based on hygiene, especially in how they disburse food and the kind of care they take relative to hygiene. The overpopulation in these two countries is another factor to consider. The incessant repetition of thought and ideas might be necessary for the apocalypse to be avoided.

The dream unfolded as such:

It was a sunny day. I walked along a path by a lake. Was someone following me? I turned around, but no one was there. Soon I approached a steep incline, and I was hesitant to proceed. It still seemed like someone was following me. I again looked back, and I could just make out a shadow. I became frightened.

I was undecided about what to do. Should I try to climb

the steep incline or turn back and confront the unknown image that was behind me? My body shook from the fear of the unknown. Either way, I had to confront the fear that was building in me. I tried to call Dr. Law and ask her which way I should go. Her words rang out to me: "You will be fine, Charles".

These were among her last words, which came to me just as I woke up.

I looked around and Debbie was reading.

"How long have I been sleeping?" I asked.

"About an hour," she said.

"Are we close to landing?" I asked.

"Another two hours."

"I am starting to get tired."

"Me too," she said.

I wanted to show Debbie around Kolkata. Our plan was to hire a driver to take us around the city. Debbie was happy about it, as was I. We asked the front desk to give us a wake-up call for 8 AM.

The call came promptly at 8 AM. Debbie and I took our showers, went downstairs and had a bite to eat. Our driver showed up at the appointed time of 9 AM, driving a blue Fiat.

"Where would you like to go?" our driver, Atta, asked.

"Just drive around the city," I said.

"It is a big city."

"Maybe we could go to an outside market," I said.

"Sure."

The drive through the city was informative. We noticed many people begging for food and rupees. We saw cows roaming the streets and rickshaws going all around. The traffic was getting crowded and the car horns were starting to blast away.

"Getting busy," I said to Atta.

"Yes, it is always this way."

People were buying everything from fruits and vegetables to meat. The fruits and vegetables looked good and fresh. The meat was hanging from racks, being subsumed by flies. We wondered how long it had been hanging there. We saw cow dung in the street, being picked up by Indians for cooking. We were approached by young children asking for money. We drove around and viewed some of the Hindu temples. The smog in the city set in. We decided to go back to the hotel and relax. We had been gone about two hours, and the crowds grew larger. We wished for a solution to overcrowding. Debbie could now see what I was talking about, in terms of the poor hygiene that plagued India.

There was a difference between Kolkata and Jamshedpur because Jamshedpur was a city built by Tata Corporation, a huge global conglomerate. Jamshedpur was not overcrowded to the extent Kolkata was. Jamshedpur was also cleaner and you did not see as many rickshaws or beggars. India is not the only country dealing with overpopulation. China is also trying to confront this malady.

"I can see what you mean when you talk about viruses," Debbie said, as we sipped our Indian tea.

Often times the unconscious is not my best friend. The dreams I would have often pricked my past from the snowy land called North Dakota. The "Lock the Door" dreams I would have generated the basic fear I had for so many things. This night, I would sleep peacefully, and the dream state was good to me. Bad dreams go away when you start to face them head on. This is what I have tried to do with therapy and critical thinking. You have to be smart for therapy to work, as it does entail being critical of all aspects of your personality. The education and reading over the years were paying off. Dr. Law had helped me understand the nature of myself and the past that was haunting me. On this night in India, the dreams of "Lock the Door" were not to be, but I wasn't sure if they would ever crop up again. Had I really mastered my fears?

We were married in a small chapel located on the grounds of Loyola School. There were just a few people there but that was fine with us. Raj and Sabu and their families were in attendance. Debbie wore a beautiful sari for the occasion. It was lovely. Father Larry Dietrich presided. It was a short ceremony, but it was elegant in its simplicity.

We celebrated with a big dinner afterwards at the Beldih Club. Debbie and I walked out to the pool area, and I took her in my arms and we kissed. The sun was just ending its cycle. The moon would soon be upon us and our life would unfold with the memory of today.

I was feeling happy that Debbie and I were married in India. It is a magical country we both love. It gave us both memories we would always cherish.

I wanted Debbie to see some more of India, which was why I opted to take the train rather than fly back to Kolkata. After our visit and my visit to the brewery, we boarded the train and headed back to Kolkata. There would be more to see there. I pointed out to Debbie how Indians were defecating in the fields beside the train tracks. She again could experience what I was telling her about hygiene.

"I do see what you mean," Debbie said, as we moved along toward Kolkata.

The train chugged along, stopping after each short distance to let off and pick up more people. This is one of the reasons it took so long to reach Kolkata. Always the stopping and starting was the program that was followed.

What I was seeing was so foreign to me. It was amazing to see Indian women carrying various construction supplies on their heads to the local construction site. Debbie, too, was taken aback by what she saw.

"Hard to believe," Debbie said as we moved along the tracks.

"Yes, this is what I was trying to tell you. I keep telling you about viruses and how I think they killed off the dinosaurs," I said.

"Yes, I think you have talked about this for a long time."

"I guess I am a little fanatical about it. The last pandemic was over a hundred years ago, and it killed many people."

"Yes, you have talked about that as well," she said.

"When I am in India, the idea of viruses just comes into my mind."

"I can see how you could think that," she said.

I sat back in my seat and let my mind take over. The madness of my mind would not let me rest. I am not sure I should call it madness, but rather anger at what I was seeing before me. The constant theme of change would not go away. Perhaps I was looking for Utopia. The cure we all seek, but can't express. How does one go about explaining the big idea of change that we seek? At what point does one's sanity usurp the madness which confronts us all?

I tired of this. It was all so implausible. I was sure things would continue on the same course. Institutions were too entrenched to let any kind of change emerge. The uprising would be squelched like an ant on a countertop. I sometimes find my mind succumbing to the dictates of the masses. The status quo had spoken and I felt a need to put this kind of idea behind me. It became apparent to me there would never be this kind of change taking place.

The Ganges still continues to flow. The burning deaths would repeal the moment and keep the embers of life as before. The forgotten jungle people will continue on the arrow of time. Humanity will still be gripped with the even flow of the clock. The flora and fauna of life will still reach for the sun. Without the sun, there is no life and we would slink away into nothingness and memories would become a dark void, searching for a new tomorrow. The end of it all is a fascination to behold. The sparking of life unfolding before us, as well as protons being disgorged from their place within the atom, were the thoughts running through my mind.

Decay reaps the benefits and the burning of the trees and all things go away. The nonsense ways engulfing the time and place we call home. The retrenchment to serenity we seek is before us. Forget the moment and live for today. The seconds tick away to oblivion. The big crunch waiting in the wings was another thought that was roiling up in me.

The big crunch is smiling at us now. It is playing a waiting game. It is in it for the long term. I can see it now, the smile of tomorrow is before us. The future put before our feet. The crunching, belching monster seething with the secrets that we all search for becomes a thought of tomorrow. The carrot put before our nose, pulling us into the black hole of eternity; the insane moments of today hurled off into the cosmos. The never-ending gibberish flowing into immortality runs deep in our psyche. The intelligent being shot down by uncertainty for time everlasting. Space and time joined in a singularity at the start. The evolving moments to the present seem like a different tomorrow. My mind kept churning for the answers.

Peering out of the train's window was mesmerizing. Soon I was reliving the phone conversation I had been hoping to have for most of my life:

"Hello, this is Charles," I said.

"This is Josh Phillips. How are you doing?"

It had been several months since I asked them to try and find John.

"I am doing well," I said.

"I think we have found John Alexander," he said.

"How do you know it is him?"

"After having a conversation with him, he did know your

mother and he did go to college in Minot, North Dakota," he said.

"So, where is he?"

"He is retired and lives in Los Angeles."

"Did you tell him about me?" I asked.

"I wanted to talk to you first."

"So, you must have his phone number and address, right?" I asked.

"Yes," Josh replied.

After speaking with Josh, I was extremely nervous about contacting John. What if he didn't want to see me? I wouldn't blame him after all these years.

"Hello," he said.

"Is this John Alexander?" I asked.

"Yes, it is."

I held the phone close to my ear, and I paused for a short while.

"Hello," John said again.

"Yes, I am here."

"Do I know you?" John asked.

"I don't think so."

"What can I help you with?"

"Did you go to college in North Dakota?"

"Yes, I did. Why do you ask?"

"Did you know a person by the name of Beth Smith?"

"Yes, I knew a Beth Smith."

"She was my mother," I said.

There was a pause on the phone.

"How is she?" he asked.

"She passed away a few years back."

"Sorry to hear that. So why are you calling me?"

I felt myself tense up. Should I just let it drop and move on with my life or come out with it and see what happens? The world was closing in on me. Suffocation gripped my neck. *I can't accept the upset in my life.* The decision was squarely in front of me. All the years of wonderment were about to be uncovered. The sun was setting in front of me, and I need to confront the challenge that was staring at me like a jackal in the jungle of life.

"Beth told me that you are my father," I finally said.

Again there was a pause on the phone. I was waiting for a response from him. The bottle had been uncorked and the squiggly lines in Dr. Law's office came crashing down on me. *What will be his response?* I wondered. The words finally came.

"I suppose that is possible. We were pretty close while we were in college," he said.

"I have a picture my mother gave me of when you were both together."

"I would like to see the picture."

"I will send you a copy."

"Great."

"I will also send you a picture of myself, and you can tell me what you think."

"Sure, that would be good."

After two weeks, I got a call from John, and he said he could see the similarities between us. He said if Beth said he was my father, he probably was my father.

"You will have to come and see me," he said.

"Yes. I will have to set that up," I said.

"By the way, thanks for the picture of you," I said.

My daydreaming came to an abrupt halt.

"Kolkata, next stop," proclaimed the voice on the train's intercom system.

Debbie and I were delighted to be getting settled for the night at the Oberoi. We asked for a driver to take us to the hotel. We were both exhausted and needed a shower and some food. The driver had a sign up that said "Charles Reed" and we were able to connect up. The ride to the hotel was about twenty minutes.

Just before we arrived at the hotel, a huge monsoon hit. The rain was so heavy the driver had to pull over and wait it out. It was kind of exciting to see this much rain come down. We started back to the hotel and as we approached it, there was intense flooding. It was only about a block to the hotel driveway.

"Sahib, I can't take you any further because of the flooding. I am afraid the car will stall out because of all the water."

I glanced over at Debbie and she seemed a little frightened by all the water. I sat there for a while, and asked Debbie what she thought about wading into the hotel.

"I don't know, Charles. It seems risky. What about our shoes?"

"It is just water," I said.

The water depth in front of the hotel was about two and a half feet. The water rushed swiftly, and I knew we would have to hang on to each other. The driver parked on an island away from the water. We got out of the car, and I took Debbie's hand. We splashed out, and it was a little scary. The current pushed us back, but we fought through it. Soon we reached the other side and dry land.

"Whew, are you in one piece?" I asked Debbie.

"I wouldn't want to do that again."

"I know what you mean."

We entered the lobby, and the staff could tell what we had done.

"So sorry, Sahib, we will take care of things," the doorman said.

Debbie and I went to our room and just dropped on the bed.

We were exhausted from the experience. After a brief rest, I rose up and outside our window the water flooded around the hotel area. Perhaps we should have waited for the water to subside. Anyway, we made it. The hotel staff was gracious about everything, and I would be forever grateful to them. Actually, now that the experience was over, it did add a little excitement to the trip. All in all, I thought the trip to Jamshedpur was a success.

CHAPTER 26

THE LAST DREAM

*L*iving together is one thing, but being married does make a difference. Soon, I was sleeping, and the unconscious mind took hold.

The dream unfolded as such:

"LOCK THE DOOR! LOCK THE DOOR!" sounded a frantic voice that came from outside my room. The voice sounded like my mother, like she had yelled so many times before in Dent. I walked over and locked the door. Soon there was pounding on the door. Incessant pounding and it went on for some time.

"Come out here," the voice said.

It sounded like the voice of my father, Jeff. I was frightened. I sat on the bed. Soon the pounding stopped. There was quiet. I heard laughing outside the door.

"Open the door," they shouted. "Come out."

I walked over and slowly unlocked and opened the door. When I looked outside, there was a group of people motioning me to follow them. I could not make out who they were. There was a long dirt path ahead that we all headed down. Just ahead was a jungle, like in India, and we entered it. A black and white panther watched us.

As we continued, we came upon a small, pure blue lake. The sun was at its peak. We all circled around and peered into the water. Suddenly, I could see all the people who were with me on this journey. It was an amazing sight. The people were fictitious as well as real. Some of the people I had only heard about: Debbie, my mother, Raj and Sabu were there. Captain Andy Mac and Johnnie Ray, the characters in my writings, were there, as was Dr. Law. Donnie Ray, the basketball player, and his friend Darrell, were there too. John Alexander and my friend, Irene, were also there. We all kept peering into the lake. At the bottom of the lake, we could see the image of my father, Jeff. He was waving at us and smiling. He knelt on one knee and bowed his head, and he was asking for forgiveness. Mother was holding hands with John and we all waved back. My mother cried, and I became emotional as well. At that moment, there was a gust of wind and the calmness of the lake became imbued with ripples and the image suddenly disappeared.

I woke up. It was early in the morning and the sun was starting to shine. In my heart, I knew this would be the last "Lock the Door" dream.

ABOUT THE AUTHOR

The author had the opportunity to travel and live abroad. He lived two years in India and North Dakota as a teenager. The town of Dent, North Dakota is a fictional town; however Jamshedpur, India is a real city in India and both of these are mentioned in the novel.

The book is steeped in the author's reality. Some of the writing mentioned, regarding science and philosophy are things the author believes can be applied today. For example, the author mentions Plato's allegory of the cave and he shows how this simple allegory can have meaning today.

The author's education is in economics and philosophy. He has a degree in economics with additional work in accounting and mathematics. The author is a CPA.

Additionally, the author's interest in the last number of years has been in the field of physics. He has been especially interested in the field of elementary particles.

D.R. Scribner

ACKNOWLEDGMENTS

The writing of the novel was done over a period of several years. I would like to give high praise to my wife, Susan, for helping me with the editing of the story. Her devotion has kept me grounded during the writing process.

The author would also like to thank R. Bensko for her tremendous work in bringing the novel to its current form.

www.ingramcontent.com/pod-product-compliance
Lightning Source LLC
Chambersburg PA
CBHW051950170626
46808CB00007B/2548